REDEMPTION

THE MIKE PARSONS TRILOGY

MALCOLM
TANNER

Publishing Coordinator – Sharon Kizziah-Holmes
Cover Design – Jaycee DeLorenzo

Paperback-Press
an imprint of A & S Publishing
A & S Holmes, Inc.

ISBN -13: 978-1-951772-11-6

DEDICATION

I dedicate this book to my wonderful wife Sandy who has encouraged me to write. She has been my strength and my hero through this process. I could have never done it without her.

ACKNOWLEDGMENTS

Thanks to Alicia Green for the use of her poem. It was very instrumental to the character, Allison Branch. Thanks to Linda Knight and her editing. She has taught me much about writing and the reader's point of view.

Thanks to Sharon Kizziah-Holmes, at Paperback Press, for the great interior design and formatting of this edition.

Thanks to Jaycee DeLorenzo, at Sweet-n-Spicy Design, for the beautifully done cover for this edition.

CHAPTER 1

*I*t seems all too unreal when it happens. "It only happens to others," is my thought. That day in February, 2010, the day my ex-wife committed suicide, lives in me now just as it may forever. It was a story that needed an ending, so that I could move on, but moving on seemed to be so much like walking through river bottom mud in work boots. My mind wanted to go where my heart may never be able to go again. I am awkward. I am strange. I could never be in a relationship again. It is my demon and my struggle. I just fail at relationships.

My forty years encompass a lifelong history of many ups and downs. At this moment, my penchant and lust for life fades into these white walls. Not even the fluorescent lighting and the strong bleach smell of the hospital can awaken me. Depression and loneliness grips me. Fate hangs over me like a cloud about to pour buckets of cold, stinging rain down *upon my head. I got what I deserved in this life. Some of it good, some of it bad, but I needed to have a better way, a better life without the anguish and torment. In life we need to make the most of our chances to be happy. The shadowy grey cloud of bad luck, bad choices or just bad karma hangs over me and covers me with a sense of deep depression. I concentrate too much on the bad, never stopping to feel the good. My choices produced this depression and led to my search for something better.*

Being an ex-prosecutor had its good and bad points. Being an ex-husband had its disastrous points. Drinking often and carousing the bars forced my attention on the negative of being a prosecutor and the disaster of my marriage, eventually leading to the end of both. It was that way before we were married. A few good drinking buddies and I made the pact that never again would we be married and "tied down." We had more fun than we could expect. Drinking and chasing women had become a hobby for me while trying to keep up with my cases, something that I did not succeed at doing. New women with no strings attached. Spend the night at their place and get back in the condo by 5 AM ready to be in court the next day. No harm, no foul right? Shave, shower and shake off the hang-over. There was no such thing as commitment. The women were in the office, in other attorney's offices and for that matter, other female attorneys, and easy to find if you wanted. I spent a lot of time away from home. I hid these encounters from my wife. That's what all guys do right? My career was more important. I was selfish. My buddies said nothing. We protected each other and worked within a silent code. I had their back and they had mine. Being an ex- husband carries with it the loss of friends, loss of home, loss of money and a loss of direction to do what you think others want you to do. Sex was for fun in my book, nothing more, nothing less. Relationships were a thing of the past.

But there are always strings attached in all relationships, right? "Be rest assured that your past will always find you out" my father used to say. There is always a ghost, always some skeleton in the closet that appears and at the most inconvenient time. Strike me down for thinking this way. It had happened before, it would happen again.

Sitting in the emergency room, thinking, I knew I had lost something when she divorced me. I could not grow up enough to understand the meaning of my responsibilities as her husband. She got the house and everything else important in my life. Our lifestyle was okay but not the one she wanted. Financially we could have what we needed but not what **she** wanted. She needed security and someone home with her every night. I needed a faster pace. I hung out with friends, my friends got married and now there is just me and other strangers in the bar. My days are more alcohol, more women, and more depression. The women are bar flies, no one special, a friend of a friend looking for a date. At forty, I am still attracted to women, but never really wanted any of them to put their shoes under my bed.

I can't remember when it started. Since the day she walked out of my life, I was becoming very awkward, so very damn awkward. Then she began to see just friends, mostly women. I truly felt at that point she was finished with men. She seemed more comfortable around other women. Life was so far from what I expected. I thought there would never be anything good happening to me.

CHAPTER 2

*I*n the hospital I wait. How in the hell did I get
here and why? What past events took place that
causes me to be here in the hospital worrying
about my ex-wife's fight for life? Snow is gently
falling against the soft moonlight as I stare out the
window. It numbs me as snow usually does. It causes
me to stare out into the open whiteness with a dull
look, often numbing my sensitivity. The white lights
of the hospital parking lot point out small white
flakes as they fall to the ground. The white blanket
then became a dull aching feeling as I stare at it. I
began to think that this night was not going to end
well. Something about impending doom always
makes you try to repel it. You try but somehow you
know it can't be stopped.

*My mind was numb and as I stared out the
window, I drifted back to another day, more peaceful
and content. The relationship of father and son
connects with my father, his father and those*

relationships as well. My mind is drifting... thinking... remembering.

"Pull your hands back, and keep your chin on your right shoulder. Now, concentrate on the ball. Ted Williams said he could see the seams rotate on a baseball because he concentrated that hard".

My dad kept telling me that if I concentrated like Ted Williams that I would someday be in the Big Leagues. My dream, my hope, and my every wish were riding on the back of his lectures, his demonstrations, and his careful attention to the details of every baseball fundamental I ever practiced.

He threw another pitch and I slammed another line drive to left field.

"Atta boy, Mike", he said. "You have to hit a lot of balls. Guys say they used to hit 'til they had blisters." Crack! Another liner, this time to center.

After a hundred pitches I am sure my dad's arm felt like a lead weight. But he did it, almost every summer night after working hard all day in construction. He kept throwing to me. He had high hopes...very high.

My dad's step-father was a tough construction worker who boxed on the side. He was a large imposing guy with huge hands that looked like two hams. There was not much fat on him at all. He was tough on my dad is the story my father told me. I always felt from listening to my dad's stories that my grandpa was the reason Dad joined the Navy. He needed to get away from him. He left and was involved in the Korean conflict. After his tour of duty, he came home and married my mother.

My mind snapped back to the stark reality of the emergency waiting room. The doctors and nurses entered the room and all were busy working in this emergency room of St. Luke's Hospital. The nurses all look the same to me, seemingly appearing nervous and anxious, yet diligent in their duties as they rush in and out of our view. I am sure they are ordinary people with ordinary lives. I wondered where they came from and what they did for fun. What was their past? Regardless if I knew their thoughts or not, I wanted them to help Sheila's parents make this thing right for us. I just wanted this to be a dream. I never wanted to be where I am now. Why couldn't I have had what I so desperately needed? But I was a grown-up now, not a child. And this is no game. Sheila's life was hanging in the balance.

My mind began to drift again. Sheila and I were no longer together. We had divorced after seven years of a difficult marriage. We had no children. Sheila could not conceive. She always wanted kids and maybe this is why the marriage faltered. It's as if kids would make it better. It was not a fit for me or her really. Sometimes you just roll on from high school and never look beyond it to find your own identity before looking for a life partner. Dating your high school sweetheart carried with it the expectation that you would marry. All your friends and all her friends kept egging it on until you just gave in saying "it was meant to be, it was our destiny". Destiny was not something I believed in. Our classmates told us that we were meant for each other. We had our good days and our good times, but the last five years or so had been tough. We started becoming poison to one another. Through law work and the hours it took, our marriage suffered due to my inattention to my wife and the home. I never got the chance to be Ted Williams or remotely close to him. But I did enjoy a nice college baseball career and few professional minor league years. But, my dream, and my dad's dream were not to be. My father and I both sulked in the loss of that dream for a while, another reason for my marriage failure as I refused to let go of baseball. I somehow blamed Sheila and our difficult marriage for my own failures. I decided if I could not play sports for a living, I would at least try law school, which I felt I would be good at. With a lot of hours spent looking for perfection that I could not accomplish as a player, maybe I could be a top-notch attorney. Good was not good enough...perfection was the goal. Sheila did not like that time spent away from her. She felt neglected and did not understand this life of interviews, depositions and courtrooms...she was tired. She dealt with me being gone when I had big cases and she was tired of the staying out late bit. And I didn't see it, just kept going my own way, drifting further away from her. Caring less and drinking more......

The doctor came through the double doors and I knew as soon as I saw his face that something terrible was happening. Impending doom was staring me right in the face and I knew something I was about to hear would stay with me forever.

"I am sorry Mr. & Mrs. Linhart, your daughter did not survive," the doctor said.

Her parents were devastated. From that moment forward, life would never really be the same for them or for me. It would spiral, twist and turn in ways I could never imagine. I hugged my ex-mother-in-law and pulled her and her husband Jerry close to me. The tears on Jerry and Margaret's face are ugly streams of water that I wished would go away. *Why are we here...why? Such a terrible thing, this is a waste of a life. Is it my fault? What in the world did I do? The divorce, the not being home, the not caring...*

CHAPTER 3

W e are leaving the hospital together, her parents and me. I begin to think of what this means, not really concentrating on where the cars are parked, just walking in that general direction. My footsteps were empty, crunching sounds that bit into our silence. We drove separately to the condo, and on the way, I could not even listen to the radio. Silence seemed to have a calming effect. *My thoughts drift again when I got back to the condo. The funeral home will be next. The funeral, the burial, so much to do and yet why am I involving myself in this?*

My life was and still is exposed to good and bad. The true good things that produce joy were in relationships. Relationships with my family are a joy, my mother and father, my brother and sisters. These relationships were steeped in family pride. That pride was developed by two loving parents, from whom I learned much. They touched my two sisters and brother in ways that we may never realize. Their influence was evident in following the family and life rules, trusting each other and always striving to be good at what you do.

I remember the tough life lessons that were learned through a diligent father and loving mother. They understood that life was not easy and the road to your happiness is covered with bumps and hurdles that sometimes made it very difficult to reach your destination. Sometimes understanding that doing the right thing is much more painful than doing what is wrong.

The problem was I couldn't follow the rules. I always seemed to have an aversion to rules. Life was to be lived without them. Fun is the goal, not depriving yourself of something you wanted because of a conscience on your left shoulder. I was nice to people, a good friend, but I was finding out my thinking and judgment were not as good as some people possessed. I was not the solution for Sheila that she needed.

I got punished for breaking rules. The punishments my parents handed out were always well thought out and conceived together. One parent never disputed the other's authority. I had great parents, a tough yet caring father and a mother whose kindness could salve any wound. I never would complain about my upbringing, as I had all I needed. But the expectations were high. We were not rich monetarily, but we were rich in many other ways. I don't think they raised their kids to make mistakes. But I did, and when I did they were there to stand by me. They did not agree with me nor did they justify what I did, but they supported me in my healing from what happened and redirected me in my future endeavors. I just kept screwing up all the time. *I didn't want to have expectations, and I had lived through expectations. Now I was going to drown in my emptiness- get vacuumed up in the dark tornado of activity that would continue to drag my life down. They must have been disappointed in me.*

I believed this because Mr. Impending Doom always found me. I can't hide. Just when I think I am secure, I mess it up again. You know how some people say there is a dark cloud of bad karma following them around?

My Karma is near...very near.

CHAPTER 4

We got home to my condo on the south side of Milwaukee. My ex-wife's parents were there with me and the awkwardness of the situation baffled me. They always liked me and we stayed in touch. They did that because I think they still felt guilty that we split. I got ready to shower and then I would make my way downstairs and begin the next really awkward scene in my life.

The shower water felt good and it began to relieve the tension I felt it in the back and neck. I begin to talk to myself again and think of my in-laws and Sheila. I thought of what I am and what made this happen. I resented this, but still felt like I deserved this. I was wondering if there was ever going to be redemption for someone like me. Or, was I just bound to a life so insecure, so rotten, that I would never again understand what it is to truly be a good person.

Jerry and Margaret Linhart are good people. I suspect Sheila was too, but I never could make myself feel the way I did about her when we married. Our relationship went flat due to the fact we just couldn't find that excitement in one another. I felt trapped and possessed. I could not feel the things a husband should feel. I felt that there was no way out. I imagined a different life than this and most of it did not contain a spouse. I wanted freedom to live without a watchful eye. I had the need to choose the activity for that day without consulting someone else. But I wanted that at one time, didn't I? Or did I?

One thing led to another, and the crisis that couples feel before divorce was starting to rear its ugly head. We fought often and argued about a wide range of things like money, sex, and, of course, my drinking habits and friends. After a brief separation, that we decided was best, we still felt like the marriage could be saved. I was a miserable husband. I just could not connect with Sheila.

I was paid back when Sheila had an affair. For everyone I never told her about, this was her way of paying me back. We were done. We were finished. After twelve years of trying, we called it quits. My thinking was, "*okay, we both had affairs, so we're even.*"

As I am dressing, my thoughts almost instantly turn to self-blame. This is my fault, not hers. Her parents will blame me and I would accept it. I will then drown in more booze and be a miserable soul, still hanging out with the barflies. I have to make my mind stop. I have a way of doing this self-drowning thing. I am a person that can easily fall and keep falling. I have things to do. I need to help my ex-in laws get over this. The voice in my head kept saying, "your fault, you bastard, you were too selfish, couldn't give, you had to have it your way...bastard!"

Funny thing though, Jerry and Margaret never

did blame me. Never once. I was waiting for it but they never did. In fact, it is quite the opposite. They still want to have a relationship, and they want to help me. I guess they kind of want to reclaim me and make me what their daughter wished I would have been. I will show them I am worthy of redemption. I will show them I am capable of more and their daughter just blew me off. They were right to not be bitter at me. She had the damn affair, not me...oh wait, Mike, you did have one and you had more than one. They didn't know about any of them, mine or hers, but I think they knew when the marriage began to go south.

Jerry is a baseball fan, so the fact that I played ball made him like me. He came to many of my games in high school and I always felt he picked me for a son-in-law long before I ever proposed. But now this event had some new feelings coming from Jerry, as though I could sense his disgust with me and was trying much harder to dislike me. This tragic event would most likely raise those feelings. Jerry was a CEO of a manufacturing company, he had money but I never wanted or took any of it. It was my rule, and Sheila abided by it, although many times I think it would have made life easier. Jerry ran on a busy schedule but yet was a doting father when it came to Sheila. He had higher expectations for her and saw the money light come on for her when I got the Prosecuting Attorney position in Milwaukee. After my failure as a prosecutor and our rapidly failing marriage, Jerry was more indifferent to me. It was like I was the bad wart he couldn't get rid of. Margaret, the always stay-at-home mom, felt like I was her project, and I guess I would always be that. After my mother had passed, Margaret took on that role, trying to reclaim any good she saw in me. Her husband was treating her differently these days. It was hard to figure, the change in his behavior was noticeable. Marriage was supposed to be long term and there were rough spots along the way. But how did I know that? I couldn't understand the right things to do myself.

Jerry called up to me from the kitchen and asked if they could get me anything. I wanted a scotch, a stout one. I wanted to stare out of the balcony window in the back of my two-bedroom condo and think of what happened in that one life, that fragile life, that I must have screwed up somewhere. But a scotch sounded good and I told him I would get something when I came down after my shower.

I ambled down the steps slowly and met Jerry and Margaret's eyes as I went to the liquor cabinet and poured a scotch. The liquor began to take out the sting but the words would not come to me...*so awkward.* They want to talk, they want to grieve. I want to be alone and drink. I didn't know if I was up to this task, they had just lost a child. *So awkward.* Children should never precede their parents in death. I have to do this, I have to try and recall every good thing I could about Sheila. Just for their sake. Jesus, this was *awkward.*

"I'm sorry, this loss is tragic. I cannot imagine how you feel. This talk is so ...awkward. I am left searching for the right words." I said trying to say it just right. "I'm so sorry, it was me, all me. This would not have happened if I had stayed. We wouldn't be here right now." I said as I genuinely began to feel my eyes getting teary. "Sheila was a good person and a loving wife. We made our mistakes and I am so sorry for that."

I did not mean to hurt anyone and people always tell you, "It's not your fault, old boy, chin up, chest out, tomorrow you will be okay." But tomorrow this would not be okay or the next day or the day after that. Now you are going to live with this thing, you bastard, and it is not going away. They don't know what we really went through. They only knew what Sheila told them. They only knew her side of our story. I think Margaret knew more than she told Jerry, but for sure, this is going to be something I will have to shoulder. It would be something that will block me from other relationships. Sheila tried to move on, but that didn't work out either. It still kept coming back to me.

"It's not your fault, you know, Sheila had issues," Margaret said. "Sheila was having a rough time, not just with the divorce. Next, she had her failed relationships. The job was becoming a handful and her work hours had been cut," Margaret said as tears began to roll down her cheeks. "She was calling me once or twice a day crying. She seemed fearful of something, afraid. She seemed scared." Margaret was near breakdown mode and I moved over and placed my hand on her shoulder. She placed her hand on mine and began to weep incessantly. Jerry came over and held his wife as she sobbed and asked "why" over and over. Tears were flowing out of Margaret's eyes and this was getting harder by the moment. Jerry just kept holding her and staring out the window as our conversation continued.

"You see, she had a stalker," Margaret said. "It was not your typical male stalking a female type, but a female stalker. Female stalkers are much more in the minority as the detective who investigated stated. Sheila was pretty sure the stalker was female. She received letters, calls, and gifts. She knew it was a woman's voice but it was so hard to believe. The story just didn't seem to make sense. She told the police but they could do nothing about it. No leads, no clues, throw away phones and no prints on the notes. The detective was a female, tall lady with blonde hair around her mid-forties, I am guessing. Very hard working and she was trying so hard to solve this stalker thing. She worked a month straight with no days off trying to find a clue on what was happening. Someone out there pushed Sheila to this. Someone knew she had weaknesses and preyed on her. The notes left on her door were threatening, ugly, and un-traceable. No prints, no handwriting, just manufactured notes of a very threatening nature. It became obsessive."

Jerry broke in, "Look, Mike, she had been going out. Hanging out in bars. Sometimes men and sometimes *not* men. She had a couple close friends who are women that I am suspicious of. One was that Jackson girl, Brenda from high school. They were "out there" in their lifestyle. Anyway, a few were, you know, well...funny." Jerry was old fashioned enough to not be able to say gay, lesbian, or homosexual.

"I see", I said pondering that thought. *Sheila never seemed to like sex. She was very inhibited and it was a lot of work to get her to experiment. We had ok but not great sex, actually, the few times it did work out. I found her to be mostly emotionally inward throughout our marriage. She told everyone in the world she loved me except me. She kept her thoughts to herself, in a private box never to be opened. I just couldn't see her taking that life change. But then again...maybe.* "Well, okay, but still why? Why did she do it?" I asked.

"I can see the cause being her depression, but I think it was more the pills and the addiction to them that caused that depression," Jerry stated as he offered a kind of sideways glance, one that made me feel uncomfortable. It was if he was accusing me with

his stare. *The wart he can't get rid of...*
"These women, you said one may have been that stalker? Do you know which one? Maybe we could ask her what was going on, what Sheila talked about." I said.

Jerry broke in and declared, "The voice was disguised, but Sheila knew it was a woman, I never really met any of them. She kept to herself about it until she started getting the calls."

"What about friends, other men? Were there any leads there? What about the detective?" I asked.

"She said she would follow up if we had any more leads," Jerry said.

He looked up at me with that same questioning look he was throwing my way before. I don't care for that at all. He was making me feel more guilt again and I guess you could say it was hard to evade.

"Do you have the detective's card?" I asked Jerry firmly. "I'll call her tomorrow."

Jerry pulled the card from his wallet.

"Hmm, Detective Allison Branch from Milwaukee. I will follow up on this."

I finished my scotch as her mom and dad reminisced about her younger days, painfully talking about the early times of our marriage. There were many tears and stories of her childhood. They left at 2:00 am.

It was hard to sleep. I could not see my ex-wife being lesbian or even trying it. Maybe it was why she was so inhibited. She was confused, maybe? I rolled over and saw 5:00 am and got back up to make coffee.

Two days until the funeral. But what about this detective? I really will follow up, I am curious...Detective Branch...who were those friends of Sheila's? Why did this happen? I needed to know.

CHAPTER 5

Allison Branch is a tall, long legged, forty-something detective. Her features are soft and pretty but there is something about that face that shows a slight lack of confidence. Her eyes were her most fantastic feature, seeming to draw you immediately to her. She carries her confidence on the outside but has a way about her that makes me think she has issues on the inside. It's as if her smile is a façade on the outside, covering for a wealth of situations and past experiences that lives inside of her, causing her anger at some junctures. I wait on a bench near the counter. The funeral had passed a week ago and I called to arrange our meeting at the precinct. Plenty of thoughts run through my mind, but I was figuring this detective to be a short, gruff, hard-nosed type, but I was not expecting her to look this good. She came around the counter to greet me. She held out her hand somewhat reservedly,

"I'm Detective Branch. Please follow me to the

conference room. I understand you have a few questions."

"I'm Mike Parsons. I'm pleased to meet you. As we have discussed, Sheila's mom and dad said you worked her stalking case."

"I remember you, Mr. Parsons, you used to be a prosecutor here, right? Sheila did talk about you some during the investigation. It sounds to me like she still had a thing for you," she said as she paused for a few moments. "I'm sorry", she said blushing slightly, "please sit down here. I am sure this has been a difficult time for you. Like some coffee?"

"Sure, been a long few days. If she did have a thing for me, she sure didn't show it. We talked some but I haven't heard from her in a year," I said with genuine concern.

She walked over to the coffee pot and poured a cup for me. As she strode back to the table and set the cup down I couldn't help but notice how smoothly she walked and carried herself. I thanked her and began to get right to the point. *She walked around like she was at home, like she belonged everywhere on this earth. She had a certain style and grace in that walk. It could not be mistaken for just good coordination. It was classy.*

"Listen," I continued, "I had lost touch with Sheila for the past three years and we didn't talk much. Our divorce was difficult. She blamed our break-up mostly on me. I could understand that, but we didn't have long conversations when we talked in the early years after the divorce. She called sometimes but the conversation was always about reconciliation or reunification. It was more as if we just needed to see each other and things would reconcile. As for still having a thing for me? I don't think so. She gave up after a while even discussing reconciliation and then she didn't call much anymore."

"Not the best husband in the world, huh?" she inquired.

"I wouldn't win any awards," I quipped.

"Did you suspect depression or her wanting to hurt herself?" Detective Branch asked.

"Not really, just kind of a blank dullness. I was there on the phone but she didn't really talk to ME, it was like she was talking to someone else. She was distant but I wouldn't have called it depression but more like in another place. She was just not herself. I saw her change in the way she said things to me. I used to feel that maybe she missed me. I relented and we went on a few dates, usually dinner but it never wound up sexual. But I couldn't see trying the dating anymore so I refused a few times and we talked less and less."

Branch continued, "When I talked with her, I thought she recalled you quite fondly, as a matter of fact. Saying things to me about how she still loved you and wanted you back. This stalker was scaring her and I think she was missing the security. Hanging out with the gay women was different for her but she was experimenting, not sure if she truly felt that was her answer in life. I thought of talking to you during that investigation, but her parents and Sheila thought you were not involved since you two weren't talking anymore."

"Did she mention these women she used to hang around with?" I said. "Where were they from?"

"She did. They were friends from high school. The one who was the closest to her was Brenda Jackson. I interviewed her and she gave us no real leads on a stalker. I was assuming she went to downtown to go out. She remembered one night at a downtown bar she thought she caught a woman staring at Sheila. It made her uncomfortable. She was with some other friends and so the others hardly noticed. Sheila was new to this group. She told me she felt like she wanted to try going the other way, but also felt some discomfort trying this out. She said she was tired of being hurt by men."

I studied her as she spoke. I couldn't put a finger on it, but I thought I saw someone I knew in her face. Truly that couldn't be, but something...

"So, this girl, did she ever see her again?" I asked.

"She said no, but she had a strong feeling that the girl staring at her was her stalker. She couldn't deny that gut feeling thing. She just glanced at her so her description was sketchy at best. We talked to the bar owner and he recalled nothing."

"No leads at all?" I inquired.

"I asked all of Brenda and Sheila's friends and they couldn't give me anything. We checked the video surveillance cam and could not put the face with the name," Branch replied.

"Sounds like you're at a dead end," I said.

"Look, Mr. Parsons, I am sorry about your ex. No matter what you feel now, you still must hurt from that loss as she was a part of your life."

"Thank you. Yes, I do, but I also hurt for my ex in-laws who lost their daughter. They are going through a tough time. They need for me to be supportive and help them find out what happened. They know her life was a mess, but mine is too. I am just trying to help them get closure, and for me, I just have to know what I did, if it was my fault, I will carry it with me. I just need to know."

"If you hear anything just give me a call," said Branch. "Here is my card."

She handed me her card and I then gave her a number where I could be reached. We shook hands and as I watched her slowly walk away, that confident air and that confident walk, the questions, why? why? It kept ringing in my head. Maybe this woman could help me figure this out. She may be too busy to help. I did know that I really want to talk to her again. I want to get this right in my head. But yeah, I want to see her again...but do I know her? She seemed so familiar.

CHAPTER 6

Unforgettable, that's what you are...
Unforgettable though near or far...

Driving to school later, the old Nat King Cole version of "Unforgettable" was playing on my CD player. I am an oldies music junkie. I go back in time to what I heard growing up or what I remember my folks listening to. The tunes are timeless and have meaning for me most of the time. What is it about a song, a certain song that just reminds you of someone? It was 4:30 in the afternoon when I got home and I dialed the number on the card Branch had given me. She answered quickly on the second ring.

"Detective Branch" answered the voice over the phone.
"This is Mike Parsons again. Hope I am not interrupting? I was just wondering if you might have a

few minutes to talk with me. Something kind of strange happened today. I just wanted to see if this helps in any way," I said.

"Sure, go ahead, Mr. Parsons," said Detective Branch.

"Well, the other day I was coming home from school. I was driving past a restaurant on West 5th and some person walked right out in front of my car. As I laid on the horn and shook my head at the person, they continued on. I noticed the person had a black hoody on and I couldn't see their face, but when I started to drive away, I noticed a red, sporty car on Elm to my left taking pictures of me. I kept driving on and it didn't make sense to me until I thought about it later. The person in that car had on a black hoody and ball cap. The person walking in front of me had the same, sunglasses, ball cap, and hoody. I didn't get the connection because I never thought it was a big deal until putting that together. Two people in black hoodies, sunglasses, and ball caps watching me. It was too strange to be coincidence. They weren't large people, actually small in stature. I was thinking maybe the stalker? Or stalkers? Then again, maybe nothing.

"Well, could be nothing," Branch said. "Like you say, it could be something worth looking into. If you see anyone following you, give me a call."

"Alright," I said and hung up the phone.

Right, could be nothing...but then again it might be something worth looking into. Give me a call...yeah, give me a call...give me a call...the words rolled off her tongue...Damn me anyway!

CHAPTER 7

Sunshine, blue skies please go away.
My girl has found another and gone away.
With her went my future, my life is filled with gloom.
So day after day, I stayed locked up in my room.
I know to you it might sound strange.
But I wish it would rain.
...By the Temptations

After talking with Detective Branch, I thought of contacting Brenda Jackson myself. I remembered her from high school and she was good friends with Sheila. I always thought she was different. I recalled how she drifted apart from Sheila as we began to date more in high school.

Brenda was an athlete in school, not gorgeous by any means, but had average looks and build. She was the funny friend, the one that always said things as a clown or a joker. She always kept her hair short, not really in tune with the times. She was friends with most everyone and never seemed upset about anything. People, like Brenda, sometimes hid deeper problems by being the cheerful clown. I always felt that way but never asked just what it was on the inside that got to her. She covered well.

Margaret and Jerry could get me her number. I wanted to talk to Brenda and just see what happened in her life and why she chose the life style she had. Not to be rude at all, I was just curious.

Driving home, I was listening to **I Wish It Would Rain**, *by the Temptations. I remembered the song from high school when Sheila and I started this on again, off again, relationship that carried on that way through marriage. I remembered a few times after our break-ups, that I became the lovesick puppy, when my girl dropped me, because I talked to someone else.*

Cue up **My Girl**, *or* **I Wish It Would Rain**, *those were the ones that could make me stare out the window and miss my girl.*

I got home from my teaching law classes at the local university and dropped the keys on the counter and began going through the mail. Nothing really important, just something addressed to me with no return address. I placed it on the counter and picked up my cell and dialed Margaret.

"Hello?"

"Hi, Margaret. How are you guys doing? "I asked.

"We're getting through it, Mike, but every day there is something, some challenge, something that brings Sheila to mind." Her voice sounded weak.

"I am sure it's hard. Anything I can do, just call. I wanted to also ask you something. Do you have Brenda Jackson's phone number? I was going to call her and try to see if she would meet me. Just to talk and maybe find something out."

"I know the detective talked to her but she really gave no indication that she knew anything, but I will get you the number. Here it is, 414-663-2772." "Thanks, Margaret, I will let you know how it goes if she will even meet with me. I just thought it was worth a try." "Mike, see if you can talk to Jerry when you can. He has been acting so out of sorts. I believe he has something on his mind. We're struggling as husband and wife because of it. Could you try to do that for me, please?" "Sure, I will. I'll do that very soon."

I went on to bed after watching the basketball game for a few hours. I set the coffee brewer for 5:00 am, my usual waking hour.

I couldn't help thinking about Margaret and her weak voice. What was going on with her? Something was telling my gut that there was something wrong with the relationship between her and Jerry. I don't know what it was but it was something. It was my last thought before I fell asleep.

I got up at 5:00 as usual and shower and dress. Drank a few cups of coffee. I took the number and the piece of paper it was on and put it in my wallet. It was 7:30 am and I'm ready to get to work. I remembered I did not open the envelope on the counter the last night when I checked my mail. I looked at it again and decided to just take it to work with me. I would see what it was later. Right now, I had to get going. I put the envelope in my satchel and left the house.

As I drive, the song, *I Wish it Would Rain*, by the Temptations, played on my CD player. *I let music depress me sometimes, preferring some of the sadder songs of an older vintage that take me to my favorite place- self-destruction. I begin to think of a time when Sheila and I were first married. I was in college and she wore a yellow bikini to our apartment pool. She really looked good. We had a couple of beers and were relaxing, taking it easy. It was kind of like a picnic at the pool. We talked, we laughed, times were good then. She worked for a law firm in town and I was a student and played baseball. I worked in downtown Milwaukee stocking orders at a warehouse at nights, weekends, and summers. This was one of our few free days. It was a day I thought that everything would be okay, we had only been married a year. We thought of children and when that might be possible for us. We dreamed of having maybe two or three, but right now was not the time and she knew that as well as I did. It was one of those "good" days we had. Days when I felt I loved her, days when I just wanted her. The day ended as we both wanted it to. Retiring back to the apartment, falling into each other as we tended to do early in our marriage. Feeling deeply, feeling like I wanted her, she went through the ritual, the foreplay, and then the actual act of sex got...awkward. She got stiff and inhibited. It was strange, and it was to be like that many other times. A good, conservative girl sometimes has that problem, my friends would tell me. To me, it was not a joke. It became more of a problem and, little by little, frequency lessened and then finally the loss of interest, then nothing... "I know to you, it might seem strange, but I wish it would rain."*

Knowing unhappy times well, I considered those days and how Sheila acted. But it wasn't an act, she really didn't like sex. I was torn between wondering if it was just me or was it men in general. She flirted some, so maybe it was me.

This thought process was beginning to consume

me. It was taking up my waking hours, causing me to be so reflective, digging deep inside of myself to find one thing that would help make this all something I could understand. Going back to immature years, youthful times when I thought I could fix everything between us was getting to be painful more than helpful. I began to pick on my own faults and inability to fix our marriage. I began to wonder when it was, exactly, that I let go. When was the time I decided the effort was not worth it anymore? What exactly did I say or do, or for that matter, what I did not do that made us drift apart? For every one point of justification, I found two points of blame. These thoughts were beginning to bring me down...

CHAPTER 8

I got to school around 8:00 am. I called Brenda Jackson. She answered on the second ring.

"Hello."

"Yeah, Brenda, this is Mike Parsons. I know it's been a long time."

"I saw you at the funeral. Terrible thing for Sheila and her folks."

"Uh, yeah, terrible for all of us, Brenda. I have talked to Detective Branch. You may recall her investigating and talking to you?"

"I do, but, Mike, I have nothing for her or probably you, either. I already told her everything I know," she said with a hint of nervousness in her voice.

"I realize that, but I told Jerry and Margaret I would follow up on this. Maybe there is something, anything that would lead us to figure this out."

"Ah, Mikey Boy, being concerned now, kind of late, isn't it?

"C'mon, Brenda, you know they still called me, you

know what our troubles were. Why don't we just have dinner? Just this once and maybe catch up and see if we can get closure for her folks. I am asking just this once." *Mikey Boy pissed me off.*

"You know I always hated your sorry ass. Ever since you came into her life it was on again, off again, Mikey. I told her what you were like before, she wouldn't listen to me. But for her, for her folks, I will have dinner with you once. But like I said, there is not much more to tell."

"Okay, you don't have to like me, just meet me at O'Shea's at 6:00 tomorrow night. I'll get us a quiet table where we can talk. Thanks again for meeting me. I just have to ask a few things that maybe Branch didn't."

"Alright, I'll be there."

Click...Hmmmm

I opened the envelope in my office after teaching search and seizure law. It was just a blank piece of paper. When I unfolded it, a picture from a magazine fell out and landed on the teacher's lounge table. Face up, the picture was of a girl, about thirty-something. Her right hand was extended forward waving only one half of the peace sign. Yes, the picture was flipping me off! Scribbled on the picture were the words that drove my next two weeks. SCREW YOU, ASSHOLE! Looked like orange lipstick, not really red but orange, like a setting sun. Okay, stalker must want to play right now. Game on.

CHAPTER 9

*D*riving *home from work, I couldn't help but think that the picture was someone, someone real, not just a picture. The extended middle finger pointed right at me. The angle of the picture made the finger accusatory, it was you, asshole, YOU, you made her do it. The orange lipstick I can't place it. Why that color, why those words? Was I now dealing with Sheila's stalker and what was the reason? I left her alone for quite some time. I didn't bother her or harass her. It had to be someone close to Sheila, yet who? Brenda? Her friends? Co-worker? Call Branch, my inner self-talking voice said. She needs to see this anyway. Yeah call Branch...Yea...Branch...*

I got out of the car and headed up the walk to the condo. I picked up my mail and the morning paper that I had not gotten this morning. I ambled up the steps with my arms full and searched for my keys in jacket pocket. And then I looked up and saw it...

'ASSHOLE!' was scribbled in orange lipstick on my condo door. I put my things down and pulled out my cell phone and called Detective Branch.

"Hello, Detective Branch here."

"Hi, this is Mike Parsons, I know you're probably done for the day, but can you come by my condo, I have a couple of things to show you. A few things are getting a bit more interesting. The address is 1343 Cameron, in the Pineridge Estates Development."

"I am familiar with the area. I used to work night shift when I was a street cop. I will be there. Just give me about twenty minutes," she said.

"Okay, see you in a few."

Branch arrived right at four PM. I watched her walk up the sidewalk to the condo with a partner in tow, remembering the first time I saw her. The face this time was much grimmer, maybe determined. I greeted her with the usual "Hi, how are you?" and she seemed focused and just grunted out, "Mr. Parsons." Her partner, a male around thirty-five, had a camera with him. Both wore side arms and badges were flashing in the glow of the setting sun and afternoon shadows. Her partner took a few photos. With gloves and plastic bags, she took a sample of the lipstick.

"You know," said Branch, "this doesn't rule out a male. The lipstick may say female but that may be to throw you off. This is at least more than we knew before. It looks to me like somebody really hates you, Mr. Parsons. Someone wants to come out of the woodwork and play with your head. It sure appears you are being hunted and, yes, probably stalked."

"Well, I guess they can join the select group of those that feel that way."

"Funny," her partner quipped and she shot a grin at him.

"Like you said, you probably don't win any

friendship awards either." Branch added.

"You are doing well with your characterization of me, Ms. Branch," I said as I shot a quick look at her partner.

"Sorry, I forgot to introduce my partner, Detective Andy Marx... Mr. Mike Parsons. Andy is in the know as he worked the case that Sheila's parents brought to the department. He has some opinions on the case and he's a bulldog of a cop."

We shake hands. He looks like the guy in school you hate because he is good at every sport, has the best car, the prettiest girlfriends and lots of money. I already don't like him. For a variety of reasons, I don't like the guy. One of which is he just looks like a smart ass. The other is he has the good fortune of being around such a beauty as Allison Branch on a daily basis. It was an awkward pause, as I am thinking these thoughts, and luckily, I snap out of it and invite them inside.

Inside we went to the kitchen counter where I retrieved the envelope with the picture of the person with the extended finger.

Smart ass partner, Andy, states it appears to be the same lipstick. *Nice deduction, Captain Obvious, your work is done here...*

Branch broke in... "I think we need to take samples of both." Marx takes the picture and places it in another plastic bag for safekeeping. After discussing both pieces of evidence, Branch warned me about watching my back and the dangers of a stalker. She also gave me some tips for handling any calls or snooping on my property. She said she would question neighbors and try to find someone who may have seen something.

"I'm going to work on this some this evening, try to get a handle on your hoody folks, your lipstick person, and maybe look back at some things I was told before on the case. Any other problems, be sure to call me," Branch said. *I am sure I will, even if I don't have a problem, I thought to myself.*

"Uh, yeah, sure," I said.

They both gathered up their things and headed out towards the door. They were just about to leave as Marx walked out on the vestibule and she turned towards me and paused. She smiled first, a smile that I thought lasted longer than most, and said, "Mr. Parsons, we will get this solved. Be careful. Remember, call me."

Her demeanor was different today. It was almost too abrupt, almost entirely different from the first time we met. Maybe not 360, but at least, a 180.

I start to tell her about Brenda Jackson and how I will meet with her for dinner tomorrow night. But then again, I think...

Oh, I won't forget. I will call you. I definitely will.

CHAPTER 10

Detective Allison Branch arrived home about 9:00 PM. The long hours and a few unsolved cases were beginning to take a toll on her. She was a veteran of the force who moved quickly through the ranks to the level of detective. She was a high school tennis player that went to college to continue her athletic career. She tore her knee ligament in an unfortunate injury, chasing a passing shot, in essence, ending her career. After leaving college, she worked in an attorney's office as a secretary and became interested in the law. She went to the police academy two years later, finishing second in her class. Go figure that her partner, Andy Marx, smart ass guy, finished first.

Allison Branch was shy growing up but competitive in nature. Play her in a game of ping-pong, she is out to win; a game of checkers, out to kick your ass. She excelled at hand-to-hand combat in the academy. She was tough in many ways, yet so vulnerable in others.

She could never win at games of love and relationships. She was always the one that was hurt or invested too much. She was a victim. She sat in the kitchen with a cold beer and contemplated the case

—▲—

Marx's thoughts tried to piece some things together. *Black Hoodies, sunglasses, ball caps, orange lipstick, two people? Three? Four? Just not enough to go on here. Someone hates him. Too many questions. Someone has to give me more, I need more information. Then again, they have shown themselves, haven't they? They are getting brave with the lipstick thing. I need to check the evidence for properties of the lipstick and where that type is sold, which magazine the picture came from, and what about that old friend of hers Brenda Jackson, the one I interviewed before? Was she a liar? I need to press her a bit more, maybe she needs another visit. I'll get on the neighbors tomorrow for some answers too.* Marx was motivated, and he didn't trust Branch.

CHAPTER 11

School is kind of a drag on Fridays, as most of my work is dealing with lawyer wannabes that don't seem to like working or reading. My mind is definitely set on my discussion with Brenda Jackson. I need to get ready for O'Shea's restaurant in Milwaukee, first because it was one of my favorite places. Black and white movie atmosphere, with small, round tables. Seating two or four people creates an intimate setting with a blue waterfall in the center. I can always imagine Bogart and Bergman sitting by the fountain, refueling the old Casablanca film in my mind. The food is great and the bands with jazz and blues singers were usually top notch. I usually go there for the atmosphere and the ability to really talk to a person. Secondly, dinner was served in courses well-planned so as you could enjoy a conversation with your meal. O'Shea's is my kind of place.

I arrived at 5:30, ahead of my reservation time of 6:00 pm so that I could be served a drink by one of my favorite bartenders in town. You see I choose bars and restaurants for the people who ran them and worked there just as much as the food or drink. Katy O'Neal is a fine Irish lass of thirty-two years of age who just had a way of making you feel at home. She never pressures you to talk or have a drink faster than you want one. If you had an empty glass, she didn't wait too long to fill it. I always feel welcome there. She is one of those girls that I like talking to but never really feel interested in dating. She is attractive but I felt like I didn't want to ruin the bartender/drinking client relationship or our friendship. In my past I would have probably hit on her, but Katy is my friend and is ever loyal to me, no matter what my mood. We get along great, she never has to run me out of the bar, and I can run off the guys that make the cheap comments. We have each other's back. Katy smiles a crisp and clean smile. She has a knockout figure that is appealing and it is difficult not to drop the friend thing and go ahead and ask her out. Always classy, Katy would be the kind of girl that would always be flattering in public, but I could only imagine that she could be relentless in the bedroom. What more could a guy ask for? She had never married. She was dating a few guys but her luck was not good. They were guys who cheated on her or guys that were just not her type or just not caring enough. She would not just settle.

"What's up, Katy O?"

"Scotch and water, Mike?"

"Ah, you know my scotch look, don't you, Katy?"

"No date tonight, Mike?"

"No, just meeting an old high school friend of Sheila's."

"Damn, Mike, I was sorry to hear about Sheila. I saw it in the paper. You shared some stories with me. I won't get nosy and ask. You know me."

"Sure do, Katy, and it's what I love about you."

"Thanks, dear, now, I have a few guys from out of town over there to get drinks to. So, I'll leave you alone. You want to talk, come by. I always have a drink ready for you, Mike," she said as her blue eyes flickered in the bar lighting. She sparkles just the way she looks at you. I enjoy facial expressions, looks and body language. I am less interested in what someone says if the body language is not there. Katy just kind of gives off a glow, one that is healthy, vibrant and totally interesting. Damn, she looks great tonight. Something different about her...

"Thanks, Katy, you're the best. Those out-of-towners give you any shit let me know."

Katy flashes her grin, the one that kills most guys. We just work well together. I often ask myself, "why not Katy?" But then, why spoil a good thing, right? I have fantasized Katy as my love interest before. I never could come to grips with changing the relationship and taking it in a different direction.

I spotted Brenda walking into the restaurant right on time. Six o'clock sharp and she doesn't look half bad, for Brenda. She was very average looking in high school, but now she seems to have improved in looks. I met her and asked the hostess if we could be seated. She took us to the table I requested, one near the waterfall. I ordered a scotch and water and Brenda a glass of Chablis. We exchanged greetings and sat down to an awkward pause of about two minutes. Thank God, the drinks came or it could have lasted longer.

"You know, Brenda, I didn't want this for Sheila or her parents. It is a tragedy and I am thinking of that a lot these days. I'm sorry it happened but we lost touch over time. I wouldn't wish this on anyone, her, her parents, it's just sad. So, try to see me a bit differently if you would."

"Mike, you know my being close friends with Sheila causes me to hate you for this, but over time I will get over it. I couldn't ever see what she saw in you, but, so many times, she wondered if it would ever work again, how it used to be with you two. I just can't believe she is gone."

"I know this is a difficult time, but can you tell me just what she was doing with her life style?"

"Okay, you know I'm gay, don't you? I came out about seven years ago. Most of my friends quit seeing me. Sheila was different. She didn't treat me differently. She accepted me for who I was. We went out some with a few of my friends, to bars and parties. I started taking her to places where other friends like me hung out. She was curious but not really into it at first. She told me a few months later that she always had an urge to try to experiment with this lifestyle and was more curious than feeling it was really her. I didn't encourage and lead her, just let her experience on her own."

I choke down the scotch thinking this is not really all the stuff I want to hear, but I turned the conversation to Brenda's friends, asking if she knew if any of them hit on Sheila or was interested. Brenda looked a bit taken back by that question, but proceeded to say that one of her friends was sort of interested and tried to get Sheila to go to dinner with her. Sheila declined, saying something came up."

"I told that to the detective, same stuff," Brenda said. "Mike, it is probably a waste of time to ask me here. I still think you're a shit, a handsome shit, but still a shit. Sheila wouldn't have been in all that sort of conflict if you could have stayed with her. She was my friend in high school, I enjoyed spending time with her, even if she wouldn't choose me or any of my friends, I still enjoyed her very much. We were very good friends," she said as she started to get up from the table and leave.

"Hold on, Brenda, don't leave." I said touching her arm as she began to get up from the table. "Please sit down, there is more. Look, you know what Sheila wanted you to know. Not more than that. So, give me a break. We just couldn't be good for each other. It was becoming poison. I think you know that. I went through all the guilt feelings and, yes, I still have some. But don't walk off, I have more I want to know."

"Alright, I will listen a bit more," she said. *The look she was giving me was quizzical, not really wanting to trust me, but it's as if she is trying to fight trusting me, knowing she is going to say things that give me what I need. I can do that. I can always get women to tell me things they don't want to tell me. I chose the wrong profession as I am sure I was a psychiatrist in another life. I love the banter of clever conversation just about as much as anything. It made me feel alive. I could remember what others said, especially all the important thoughts.*

"Look, Brenda, it is important to know if there was a stalker and where to try to find this person," I said.

Brenda looked up from her glass of white with once again that same quizzical look. "Yes, the stalker existed, but there were never leads, nothing to go on. One of the notes Sheila shared with me I kept. I brought it with me." She reached into her purse and she handed an orange envelope to me. The color instantly got my attention. I opened the note and all that was in it was a picture. It shows a woman with a black hoody and ball cap, the caption underneath... "You didn't choose me!!!! You're dead!" The face is blacked out. I never turned it in to that detective. I was truly scared for her when she showed it to me.

What scared her most is where she found the note. It was under her pillow." Brenda had not touched a bite. "How could someone get into her house if she had an alarm system?" I knew she had a good one. I didn't think Sheila was careless. She had always been very careful, very fearful of burglars or intruders. In fact, she was paranoid about it. I said, "Looks like she did draw interest from somebody."

I looked at Brenda closely looking for some kind of clue or admission that she knew more, but she casually looked away and said, "Yeah, she was that way. Sort of held her feelings inside. She was so private, sometimes."

We finished the conversation and it slowly slipped into nothingness, until finally she became so quiet that both the meal and the evening were certainly almost over. I have to call Branch. I started to tuck the note into my jacket pocket but Brenda asked for it back. I started to object but she insisted. Instead of making a scene, I gave it back to her. She nodded politely, put the note in her purse and she stated that she was about to go. I asked her to have just one more drink, but wanted to excuse myself to go to the bar and order. She agreed to one more white wine.

"Meet you on the closed-in patio with two more drinks," I said as I slipped off to the bar to find my friend, Katy, the Irish lass and ask a favor.

"Katy, can I ask you to do something for me?"

"Sure, for you, anything!" she replied with the smile that would steal any guy's heart.

"I need you to take these two drinks to the enclosed patio to that lady I was with. Her name is Brenda Jackson. She has something I want in her purse. I don't think she's a good person, I wouldn't ask you to do this if I didn't really need this. She's one of Sheila's old friends from high school. I suspect her for some reason as having more knowledge of the stalking situation than she wants me to think. I made her uncomfortable and when I get back to her, would you page her to come to the bar? Tell her she has a call and then say they hung up. It will give me enough time to photo what is in her purse and then put it back in there before she gets back."

"Sure thing, buddy boy. Going to have a drink with me later when you get rid of her? Maybe I can help you figure things out."

"Anything for you!" I said. I meant to keep that promise.

I loved talking with Katy. Talking to her was like talking to one of the guys, except she was gorgeous. The thought of Katy once again crossed my mind. Why not Katy? No, I like our relationship the way it is.

On my way back to the table I was hoping my plan was going to work. Thankfully, Brenda was still waiting for me and hadn't left.

"Our drinks will be here in a second. Let's sit by the fireplace and just relax. We won't talk about Sheila anymore and we can just talk about anything," I said.

Soon after, Katy arrived with our drinks and slipped a written message to Brenda. Brenda sat there for just a few seconds with that quizzical look again, and then excused herself and followed Katy to the bar. Quickly I removed the note and took out my phone and took a quick couple of shots. I immediately placed the note back in the envelope and back in her purse.

"There's no one on the line," said Brenda suspiciously.

"You are Brenda Jackson, right?" Katy replied.

"Well, yes, but there is just a dial tone."

"Well, I'm sorry, but there was a call for you."

Katy went about her work as normal as could be

and Brenda slowly left the bar throwing mistrusting glances towards Katy a couple of times. She came back to the patio and sat back down. We sat for a while talking about a few of life's more dull topics, her life and mine, where we worked, what we were up to. I told her I am teaching law at the college and she said she works for an ad firm in Chicago and that she commutes by train. We small talked and then I walked Brenda to the parking lot and to her car, wished her a good rest of the evening and went back to drink one with Katy.

I sit on the stool in front of Katy and thank her for her help. She pours me one last scotch and a smile, and I exhaled a deep sigh.

"Want to tell me about it?" she asked.

"Well I told you that Sheila was stalked, and I think this Brenda is involved. But I need to get the information to Detective Branch, and see what she thinks," I said.

"Hmm... female detective, huh? Is she nice?"

"It's not like that, Katy. *I just lied.* I think she is good at what she does and I think she is really trying to help. I just need to solve this for her parents and for myself. Maybe the reason I am doing this is for redemption. I've lived a shitty life and want to do something right for somebody. We all need some closure on this. *Am I a liar? Or do I really feel this way?*

It was my first clue, I was trying to suppress something. Do I really want to know Allison better? Do I like her? Want to date her? Trying to deny it to my friend, Katy O'Neil? Maybe Allison already is dating Andy Marx, whom I am better looking and smarter than anyway...

"Mike, Mike!"

"Oh yeah, Katy, I need to call this detective tonight,

the info can't wait." I finish my drink, pay my bill, and left Katy and the waitress a handsome tip. "Thanks, Katy O, you were great! Love you like no other." I told her we would talk in a couple of days.

Yeah, I wish, Katy thought. Why not me, Mike, why not me? All the times you have come in here and shared with me. Who could treat you any better than me? Who, Mike? Who? You know we could have a good relationship. You know I am one of the few people who really understands you. I know your story, you've told it to me many times. I hang on each word, every time. I know you can't settle on a woman. But I could make it different for you. I could change your life. You just won't let me in. I am just your friend. Like one of the guys. I don't want to be one of the guys. I want you, Mike."

CHAPTER 12

You give your hand to me, and then you say hello,
And I can hardly speak, my heart is beating so.
Anyone can tell, you think you know me well,
But you don't know me.
Ray Charles, "You Don't Know Me"

Allison Branch's cell phone rang at 9:30 pm. She was sitting in her living room studying the file of Sheila Linhart's case.

"Hello?"

"Hello, Detective, it's Mike Parsons. I have something interesting to show you. I had dinner with a friend of Sheila's, Brenda Jackson. Something very interesting that she showed me was a note. I have a picture of it as she didn't want me to keep it. I would like to think it goes along with my door message and the people walking in front of my car. I think it all goes together, but for the first time it seems to tie Brenda in to this, in some way. It really makes me think we have a lead here."

"I interviewed Brenda and she didn't show that to me. Maybe she is hiding something," Allison said as she looked back through the questions that were asked to Brenda Jackson before. "I've got a hunch, but I am not sure. Meet me at the station in thirty minutes. I need to talk to Ms. Jackson again."

Allison flew to get dressed. She wanted to be on time, to be early. She felt her heart race some, not only because she may have a lead, but mainly because she could see Mike. She had thought of him often, too often. She had noticed Mike in some of the bars she had visited. She couldn't tell herself in an honest way that she either liked him or not, but he did occupy her mind. Allison was not sure why, if it was his smile, his way of listening or just that she was lonely. It could've been all three she thought, but she was attracted to him. It's just hard to deny that feeling. Allison Branch represses what she feels. She puts it on the back burner. She does so because she wants no part of any pain, pain like the many times men have left her empty and alone. *You know what picky gets you, don't you, Allison? It gets you loneliness. You end up like Sheila, not wanting men to hurt you. You end up somewhere else because you can't take another risk with your heart.*

She got to the precinct and as she walked in Mike was already waiting outside her office. *Cool down, Allison, don't act like a kid. You like him, yes, but don't let him think that. Damn he looks handsome...oh, stop it, just shake his hand, thank him for being here, and ask him into your office. Then get to business. Just leave it at business. You are shying away again, Miss Allison. What are you afraid of?*

"Come on in, Mr. Parsons." She held out her hand and I shook it and said "thank you," but I didn't let go for what seemed to be a very long time...*awkward...I am so awkward.* I finally let go of her hand and that song **You Don't Know Me** came to mind by Ray Charles. It was hard for me to open my mouth and reply. "Uh, yeah um, Detective I have this note I told you about on the phone." I take out my cell phone and dial up the picture I took and enlarge it for her to read.

"Hmmm," she read out loud "you didn't choose me, you're dead?" Her voice trailed off in the end and it appeared that she was studying the note rather than reading it. "Didn't choose? Mr. Parsons, tell me who do you think it might be that Sheila didn't choose."

"Well, kind of hard to say, although right now at that time in her life there was no one really serious.

"Well, you need to look at the choices. I see two things here. One, there is probably more than one suspect. I don't think this thing is limited to one person. There is more than one guilty party. And two, you must have a lot of people that haven't liked you over a lifetime," she said with a half grin. "Guess you need to determine which one of your friends is for you and which one is against you. This Katy girl, you can't rule her out either."

"Well, that may be, but Katy really is harmless. Most people I know basically took sides when Sheila and I divorced. After the lines were drawn in the sand, it seems easy to tell who's not on my side of the line," I said maybe too defensively. Most of my guy friends are still my friends. The female friends of Sheila's, not so much."

Allison looked up from her note and said, "Yeah, maybe, but you better worry about who isn't decided yet. It seems like someone is on the fence."

Allison began to think out loud trying to determine the hoody significance, the sunglasses and the ball caps, orange lipstick, orange paper, the photos. Are they photoshopped? She asked if I have had anyone on my list of girls I had dated previously from which there might have been tough break ups? Did I owe anyone money? What was the connection with Sheila and the disguised individuals? We discussed once again the significance of the fact Sheila may have been pursued by another woman.

I couldn't leave Brenda out of the mix. She was starting to look like a suspect to me. Brenda was the right height and the right build of the person crossing the street in front of my car. It could be Brenda. She just could have lied to Allison about her involvement. I couldn't really put Katy in the mix. I keep trying to think of someone in my past that could hate me or hate Sheila that much. But it isn't coming to me.

"Mike, we need to talk a lot more about this. How about meeting down at the Sidecar Bar? I see this atmosphere every day. We could both use the change of scenery. It's kind of quiet and we can talk more about who to look at as suspects. I am convinced we are missing something, but I don't know what, "she said.

"I'd love to. A couple of beers won't hurt anything, will it?" I reply to Branch, looking at her a bit longer than I needed to. Her eyes were drawing me to her again. I wish I could describe the way she looked to me with those eyes when she only uttered one word...

"Nope", she said and with a smile that goes straight to your gut. One that resides for quite a long time in your soul. One that would never go away...that's what I thought.

CHAPTER 13

We both pulled up to the Sidecar at about the same time. I waited for her to meet me at the front entrance. She had on a waist- length jacket and white blouse. The jacket was open and white shirt was cut to what I call just the right level. She dressed well and I couldn't help but notice how she didn't just walk through the bar, but strolled through it with confidence. She waved at a few people, likely friends, making me think she came here a lot. She sat at a table near a street side window and I sat across from her. We made some small talk and then focused back on our mission to, one, drink some beer and, two, to try and make some headway on why my ex-wife committed suicide. We ordered a couple of beers and by the time the waitress re-appeared we were into the conversation. I started a tab and thanked the waitress.

"Well, I still have a hard time seeing your reason for wanting to find these things out. I could understand a lot more if you had kept in contact with her or saw her occasionally. But basically, your relationship was pretty much toast from what I gathered," Allison said.

"That part is true," I responded, searching her eyes for something that explained her line of questioning, wondering what she was really after here. "I suppose I could only explain it as redemption of my own soul, defeating my own demons, for once being the hero and winning a championship instead of trying to explain away why I came in fifth place." I look away from her, out the window after saying that. I returned my glance back to her and her stare was fixed on me. It was almost as if she knew exactly what I was thinking. Somehow, she was looking hard at me to understand.

"I can see that I suppose. There are worse things to wish for other than redemption." She was not focused on the events of the past few days. She was sort of messing with my mind and I didn't like it. But at least she seemed interested.

"Detective, what is it that you make of the orange lipstick, photos, the hoodies, sunglasses and the ball caps?" I asked, changing the subject back to the events. "Did you question my neighbors and did they see anything?"

"Yeah, I put Andy on that. He asked everyone that lives near you if they saw anything. No one was around or even bothered to look out." She stated. "What I have to go on is what you saw and the people you suspect. I will get Brenda Jackson back in and ask about the note and why it was found in the house. What about Brenda's friends?"

Yeah, you should talk to them, too. I just don't trust them," I said.

"I understand." Allison took another long drink of

beer and then looked right at me and just blurted out, "Just what in the hell happened to you and your ex?"

That comment hit me in the face. I wasn't ready for it. I didn't know this was the date we got to the personal things. We weren't even on a date, were we? I had started many a relationship over a few beers. But this sit down seemed so different. I stammered a bit and then found a reply somewhere in the dark regions of my mind. Recovering nicely, I told her that we just couldn't connect, that she had tried a few alternative type dates that didn't work. I explained our marriage in the way I explain it to anyone else who wanted to know. We couldn't keep going on and we were wearing each other out. What we wanted were two different things. We didn't need each other; we needed some different types of people to be our spouses. We were harmful to each other, toxic and poison. Plain and simple, it wasn't going to work.

Branch then responded with, "That could be, but I just have to know...did you try, did either of you try? What made the poison come out?"

She was looking for one thing with this interrogation; she was looking for just one simple reason to like me, just one. She didn't care what I did before I was married, but what I did while I was still married and was my soul even halfway redeemable. Somehow, I sensed that she liked me and that we could have some sort of relationship. But there were just some things she needed to know that required a full court press from her. She pressed on.

"Did you love her before it turned sour? That also could be none of my business. I want to think the best of you, Mr. Parsons..."

"Call me Mike," I interrupted.

"Listen, Mike...I really am having a hard time trusting you, I want to, but some of this story really makes no sense, especially the note with the girl's picture giving you the finger on it."

"I know, Ms. Branch..."

"Call me Allison, Mike"

"Okay, Allison, let's just cut to the chase. You think I know these people and had something to do with the stalking. I did no such thing! Maybe you should drink a few more beers and be a bit less paranoid. I knew Brenda was Sheila's friend, but I didn't know those other women, by name, or face. So just for openers, you can rule me out because you want it not to be me anyway. So there!"

And then she does the most unusual thing for the way this conversation was going...She presses her first two fingers to her lips and then slowly presses them to my cheek.

"Good, I was hoping to do that, you are right." She got up from the table and touched my hand and then slowly walked away, right out the door, and I was thinking...*I'm so awkward.*

I paid the tab and was walking to my car and cold night air hit me in the face. I got into my car and slowly drove home thinking. I guess I was blowing it again, as my failures once again mounted up and were bringing me down. I am being quick tempered and harsh, once again, ruining my chances to be with this woman. I just can't bite the bullet and take it. I think I was feeling offended but yet wishing I had been patient.

Here I go debating with myself, once again. I was arguing with an inner voice that is two people in one. I am one who cares way too much about everything, and another that just doesn't give a shit about anything. Am I bi-polar? She doesn't trust me yet? What the hell did I do to deserve that? She was right to walk off. You shouldn't come off like that, Mikey.

I'm even calling myself Mikey now. Every time I have a chance to settle in, I just have to go off. She doesn't deserve it. She is trying to help. It is my way of pushing others away. It will only end badly, right? I finished the drive home and parked the car. I go inside, and turn off the alarm. Turn on a few lights and decide on a ham sandwich and beer to finish off the night. I turn on the Bose speakers connected to my phone. I hear Buble' singing **"The Best of Me"**. Outside it is dark and getting close to eleven. Just beyond his balcony in the bushes near the backyard fence of the complex, stood two small figures, dark hoods, and ball caps and painted white faces. He didn't know they were there. They were holding something in their hand. Looking at him through his balcony and he had no idea they were there.

Ha! "The Best of Me?" She is seeing the worst of me, my faults, and my demons are killing me. I have to be better than that. I will never get anywhere with that woman with the attitude I showed tonight. I sat on the bed thinking I should call her and tell her I was sorry for that outburst. Maybe she'll call me, maybe text me? I sat there for at least fifteen minutes debating it, but decided to turn in. Tomorrow will be another day. Don't be weak, she was interrogating you, buddy boy. Damn It, I wish I wasn't so awkward with women. It seems like the barflies are my destiny. I never will find a good one. I don't deserve one...

I laid back and fell asleep. Sleeping deeply, I was dreaming, I saw Sheila, I saw her bloated and puffy face lying inside the casket. I saw the flowers, I saw her parents and then a loud crash, breaking glass...shit! That was real! It startled me to a wide-awake mode. I grab my Luger and phone, dialing 911. Quietly, I tell the dispatcher that I have an intruder, giving my name and address. I started to move where the front window is broken and I feel the cold breeze hit my chest. I walked carefully looking for shadows or movement. I never thought I would have this happening. I have imagined it before, but it is really happening now. The last thing I felt was the blunt object that hit my shoulder as I saw the shadow and a foot. I am sure it is a foot crashing into the side of my head. I am out, cold.

CHAPTER 14

I am in a hospital room and awaken to smart ass guy, Andy Marx, looking over me. Not the sight I was hoping for. It looks like making up to Allison is on hold. My head feels like the hangover from a weekend binge drinking session. My shoulder is in a sling and not moveable. I remembered the trouble and getting up to check it out. One thing I also remembered was the moving shadows. I did not see any faces or any clothing, just dark shadows that moved...fast!

Marx interrupted my thoughts. "Glad you are with us. You took a couple pretty tough blows. Branch is over talking to your neighbors who heard and saw a few things. We might get a few leads out of it." He seemed like an okay guy, but it was my job to hate him.

"Yeah, didn't see it coming, just saw moving shadows," I grunted.

"Your neighbor who lives underneath, he heard the

crash and also called us. Funny thing, he thought you had an alarm system and he didn't hear it go off. So, he was a bit slower than you at calling 911." Marx said, as he chomped on a piece of gum like he was trying to kill it. "You know, it doesn't seem like someone wants you alive," Andy said, as he continued to smack the gum.

"Yeah, well, that may be the case. I thought sure I had set the house alarm." I said, as I looked at him through one good eye.

"It wasn't going off when we got there," said Marx.

"Shit, I always set that. What was I thinking?" *I tried to retrace my thoughts as I laid there before sleeping. Turned off the alarm...but didn't re-set it. Damn it, we might have had them. Who is we, anyway? Me and my new super hero detective interest, Allison Branch, that's who!*

"Everybody forgets sometime, my friend," Marx said. "Too bad it meant a few injuries to you. You know how to use that gun you had right? You're lucky they didn't kill you with it." Marx was trying his best to be nice about how I should have locked the door and stayed in my room till the cops got there. But I could tell he knew I wasn't in the same league with these people. There were tougher, skilled in fighting, which, of course, I wasn't, and had a mean streak that only the cops should be dealing with. He was right, unfortunately. I would never be able to look heroic to my detective interest. I would suck once again.

"Hey, Marx, thanks." I said as I started to feel nauseous and drowsy. The nurse came in to make sure I didn't sleep as they wanted to observe. Marx told me to take it easy and patted my hand making me feel like his kid brother or something and started to leave the room. He turned before he left and said, "Look, Mr. Parsons, I'm going to tell you something, be careful who you trust." His look was grim and he wasn't kidding. "Get some rest."

Why am I doing this, going through this? Is it my own redemption I want, or do I just want HER? My life up to this point seems pointless. I am searching for a way to have some purpose. I need to love and to be loved, but somehow, I won't allow that. There is Katy, my good friend bartender, cute, sassy, and has that certain flair that every guy could be attracted to. There is Branch, difficult to figure and certainly someone I could love, and there is Sheila. She is gone, she is DEAD, and my heart is just now starting to feel the pain it should when you lose someone you love. Is it for her, her parents, that I need to complete this? I can't be better until I do something for other people. My life will continue to be a pile of shit unless I get this done. Sheila once loved me. I am sure of that. Did she when she left this earth? I don't know that. I think Katy likes me...but loves me? I have often thought of Katy and having that special relationship with her. I don't know about that. It makes me a bit nervous because we are friends. The mysterious Branch looks like a hero, acts like one, too. She certainly does something to me. I just don't know what I need. I need to laugh and I need to cry. I need to go to someone and I need for them to run very far. I need someone to run to me and I need for them to run from me, too. It is confusing, it is...awkward. It is my way. I am always saying something right in the wrong way. Pissing people off when I didn't mean to. Having them fall for me when it is not the plan. I don't want plural women any longer. I don't want to try to seduce barflies. I need to be loved. I need more importantly to love, like life was intended to be. I am in this hospital, head throbbing and shoulder in a sling because I am a bad person, I am sure of it. It's what I deserve. Isn't it always what I deserve? It is what my dad said...it was his way, "You got what you deserved, no excuses. You got what you deserved. I told you not to marry her." Yes, he said that, he actually said that. In life, I never really truly measured up again. Falling short here and there, never quite making it to those high expectations. True failure. Life must change for me, it just has to. Starting with finding those son-of-a bitches that drove Sheila to her ending is where it starts. Maybe along the way I will find me, find my life, and find my purpose. Whatever I have achieved, it has never, ever, ever been good enough.

I looked up and there she was. My detective heroine. I thought she had forgotten about me and just left me to Detective Marx. But as she glided into my room, the same way she always does, that feeling of awkwardness came over me. I am grown up and not supposed to be laying here hoping for a heroine to rescue me from the evil stalkers. I felt a bit embarrassed but her voice eased my apprehension a bit.

"Looks like you took a couple of nasty shots up around the head and shoulders," as she looked down with a fantastic half grin. I was wondering if she practiced that grin. It was effective. It seemed to take away my fear for one and my loneliness for another. The smile was as if she was saying, "gee, I am happy to see you and that you weren't hurt too badly." It was what I was hearing in my head.

"Yeah, hurts like hell, but I guess I am not very awesome at self-defense. For a guy that had a gun, I should have had the upper hand."

"Well, sometimes training is good for that. I am

glad you are going to be okay. Not only do we have stalking, but now assault to go after. I talked to some of your neighbors. The two that broke into your house differed in height. Mr. Jones, in the unit across from your condo, heard the window break and called 911 about the same time you did. He saw them leaving through the broken window. Two of the figures had hoodies and painted white faces. They had ball caps and sunglasses, too. I looked at the surveillance video from the manager of the complex. Although somewhat dark, I could see the figures and got a good idea of height and weight. They ran out the back and climbed over the stone wall before we arrived."

"Hmm. Two girls? A guy and a girl, what do you make of it?" I said through a grimace I really didn't want to show.

"Well, at least one is a girl or a really short guy. Their clothes were baggy so there isn't a way to identify male or female physical shapes. If I had to guess, I'd say two women. Know any tall women, friends or enemies of yours?" she asked.

I began to tell her I know lots of females, both friends and enemies, but smartass was not the proper take here. "I'll give that some thought here in the next few days. The doctor said I should get out of here tomorrow. They just want to keep me overnight for observation," I said.

"I am going to make one more trip back and have your manager let me in your condo. I want to examine it closer. I have a couple guys over there right now taping it off. You may have to stay another place for a few days until we wind it up. Do you have a place to go?" Branch said and I thought I could see in her face that maybe I could get an invite...*uh no, keep it straight up. NO funny business!*

"Yeah, sure I got a place. I will call my brother. He

will let me stay a few days."

"Good, then we should be able to process this in a couple of days and then we can have you back in your home." She turned and as she walked away, she suggested, "Maybe you should invest in some self-defense classes."

"Yeah, if I could find a good teacher, I would give it a try." I winced once more from the headache and felt really tired.

She deadpanned looked me right in the eye and said, "I'm the best. "And she turned back one more time and smiled. Heart shot. And with that, she walked out of my life... for just a few hours.

I bet you are the best, Allison Branch, I bet you are. Hey, buddy boy, straighten up. She's different than the rest. You know she is. She would converse, keep you stimulated with her intelligence, teach you self-defense and actually love you? No, that is something that I don't know, how could I know that? Can you let her...yeah, can I let anybody do that?

Marx said... "Be careful who you trust." My last thought before sleep overcame me.

CHAPTER 15

My brother James is one of my best friends. I called him and asked if I could stay a few days while they processed my condo for evidence. He is always there when I need him, there with a joke, a smile, and a listening ear. James picked me up the next morning and took me to his place. His wife, Monica, was working, and his kids were in school, so we would have time to sit and talk. It is these times that I love my brother the most. He doesn't judge me, he just listens. We poured a couple of coffees and sat in his living room.

James began by asking the Captain Obvious question, "Just what in the hell is going on? You and I have been through a lot together. Now this assault business is getting way out there. Tell me the story. The funeral was not that long ago. You didn't have much time to get over that before you were targeted. Do you think there is a connection?"

"James, I really believe that there is. I've been

talking with this detective downtown named Allison Branch. She and her partner are processing the scene at my house. Sheila's parents contacted her with their concerns. Allison looked into the case, and didn't find anyone. Since my troubles, the department reopened the case. You know Sheila experimented with an alternative lifestyle. I think there is some connection to those friends she made. It could possibly be someone they know that Sheila didn't tell her parents about. I suspect Brenda Jackson."

"You mean Brenda from high school? I always thought she was kind of a strange duck anyway. I asked her out once and she turned me down. She always gave me the impression she didn't like guys," James said.

"Well, I took her to dinner and she had a piece of evidence, a note she didn't give Branch the first time it was investigated. I got Katy at the bar to distract her while I snapped a picture of the note. After I showed Branch the photo, she decided to call Brenda in for further investigation. I hope she gets somewhere," I said.

"Yeah, but are you safe? I don't like how all this is unfolding, Mike," James said.

I sat in silence. What was there to say? While I often confided in James, I must protect him from worry, hide him from my own fear.

"What about this detective? You talk about her a lot. You like her or something? I didn't know you were the type to fixate on one woman these days," James said.

"I do like her but she's hard to figure. I think she's a good cop and vested in the job. But, I feel like she's searching for something in her personal life." At this point, I felt an urge to reveal my fascination with this woman but thought better of it. In this early stage of infatuation, all cards must be held close. "I think she's afraid of something. This may never work out well between her and me. You know why, James? I will ask too much, want to know too much, and push her away. I will just have to remind myself that she is working on the case and I am just the victim here."

"Hey, you ought to look at Katy, man. I think she's hot in that 'girl next door' kind of way."

"Yeah, maybe. I like Katy a lot, but maybe not well enough for a long-term relationship. I wanted to take her out once, but she had something going. I didn't ask again. At times wished I would have. She hangs on every word I say. She just looks at me like she wants to possess me. I really like her, and she's very, very hot. Sometimes that makes me afraid of getting too close to her. But Branch...now there is someone that when she walks in a room, she immediately gets attention. All eyes follow her when she makes an entrance. Once you see her, you can't take your eyes off her. I think it's her eyes, although she rarely looks you in the eye. But when she does, she zones in on you. You feel captivated, even overwhelmed by her."

"That good?" James asked.

"Just that good, brother. It's the feeling that makes you ache in the gut. Almost to where it hurts. James, I got to go back and lie down. If I get in the way here, just run me out."

"You're always welcome here, brother."

"Well, Monica, may get tired of me hanging out here. Maybe I will get my place back soon."

"No hurries, no worries" a phrase that my brother always said. He never made me feel out on an island. I was always welcome in his house. It was always that way and always would be.

I went to the spare room and laid down, all the while thinking of Branch, how she looked, how she smelled, how she walked and how she talked. There was something about those eyes that locked you in to a hypnotic trance you couldn't break. Something behind the eyes yearned for something so much more than she had known. It was needy, but not deprived. She knew what she wanted.

I drifted off into a dream. I was holding her, looking at her, and gathering the courage to ask what I wanted to know. So out of character for me and so uncomfortable that I felt ...awkward. I usually didn't need to ask any questions, it was just, 'hey whatever happens.' But in this dream, I was careful. I was not sloppy, but rather cool and sophisticated. I wanted her to know how much she meant to me. You are careful to say and do all the right things when you care. It's not to impress her, but to respect her. I asked her, "Do you need me? Like the way I need you?"

Branch responds with a passionate kiss on the lips. No words, no small talk, just that 'I want you' kiss that burns inside of you when you know the relationship is working. It works because you want to give more than receive, but, mutually, you both know it's good. My arms caress her back and shoulders as we continued to kiss deeply. With my arms now totally around her, we fall together into a oneness on my bed...

My alarm on my phone is screeching. *Damn it, as I awaken, that might have been the best dream I ever had. If I could only make it come true.*

CHAPTER 16

I got dressed and left my brother's place at 9:00 the next morning. I needed to get back to school soon, but I had other things I needed to deal with. *Questions kept running through my mind. Why? Who is doing these things, and what do they have against me? I know Brenda must be involved. She hates me for a reason. Jerry? He has a reason to hate me, too. Could he? Other scorned one-night stands or temporary girlfriends in my past? I'm missing something, overlooking something...*

Pulling into the police station, I decided to see Branch. I went in the front door and stopped by the front desk to check in.

"Detective Branch, please."

The desk sergeant looked up with annoyance and buzzed Branch's office. She came out to the front to meet me. "Come on back, Mike." She smiled that smile that holds you. "Well, c'mon, are you in the twilight zone or something?"

Oh, so it's Mike now? Maybe things are going in my direction. If only my dream could come true.

We walked back to her office. She walked gracefully in front of me and glided into her office door. Closing the door, Allison offered a chair, and she began to cover the case.

"I think I have a lead, Mike. Ran into an informant who I know hangs out with a druggie crowd of lesbians. Heard of some kind of plan within her group that targeted people, a husband and an ex-wife. It fits. It could have been you and Sheila they targeted. I think it could be Brenda Jackson. She's definitely hiding something or protecting someone in this deal. I'm going to lean pretty hard on Ms. Jackson, so I want you to be careful. You don't need any more kicks in the head," Allison said.

"I know Brenda is involved," I said. "That seems obvious. But I don't think she's one of the attackers. I think she's the brains. The one that kicked me hard had to be in shape. It felt like a ton of bricks. I knew Brenda and her sister took martial arts courses, but I don't think either one could kick me like that."

Branch looked at me quizzically. "There is something more involved that we don't know. Some puzzle pieces are missing. We need the motive, which we don't have. But, we also need the plan and the main characters involved. Why did the plan develop? Who is hurt and who wants revenge?" She kept staring at me as if she thought I could fill those in. But, I had no idea where to begin. We needed a break in the case.

"Well, I can guess on a couple, but it is hard to follow this group and what was going on. My mind just can't get wrapped around who and why. I guess I could say I have made plenty of people unhappy with me on my journey through life."

"Mike, you have to look at it from the group's eyes. I feel like they have you in their sights because you represented something that held your wife back from committing to someone in that group. Maybe Brenda, maybe her sister, or maybe even someone else. But there is even more to it than that. I wondering if the drug problems in this city has much more to do with it than we think. I'm going to put Andy on this and see what he can dig up, too. It's connected. It just has to be."

I could feel my mind racing, trying to process the fact that my ex-wife could have been involved with drug dealers and homosexual relationships. She had never been that way. Just depressed and lost. I began once more to feel the guilt about that relationship. The guilt connected to her death. She is not a person to hurt others.

"What happens next?" I asked.

"Well, I'm sending Andy to investigate this group and see if we can come up with more solid information than the informant gave me. I need places they go and people they see. I feel much closer to a fight now, feel like I can get after some people and find out who is doing all this. This sister, do you know her name?"

"Her name is Breanne. She was always the little sister who tagged along with Brenda and wanted to be older than she was. Let me know if I can help."

"It would be good if you stayed out of this for now. Somewhere along the line, however, you may need to help us. I believe you connect somewhere in this case. It's not just your late ex they were after... it was you, too."

I shook hands with her and got up from my chair to leave the office, when from nowhere I just blurt out, "Let's have dinner tonight." Damn, I never do that.

Never, Never, Never. I totally was blown away when she said, "I'd like that."

"How about O'Shea's, say 7:00?"

A smile came across her face that said something to me. Something that answered my question. Something I wanted to know for a long time. I only needed that smile to know.

CHAPTER 17

I walked into O'Shea's at 5:30 to calm my nerves. I waved at Katy as I took my seat at the bar. Not too busy tonight. After work, bars were full of nerds and turds. It's why I liked this bar and why Katy was my rock. I could depend on her, she had my back. It was hard to tell Katy I had a date. Although we never dated, I knew that she liked me. The feeling was mutual.

"Hello, Katy, my fine Irish lass. How about a scotch on the rocks? I'm a bit nervous about my date."

Katy never looks at me quite the way she did when I told her that. The look was somewhat surly and with a twist of her lower lip that screamed jealousy. She recovered quickly and finished pouring my scotch.

"So, is it the detective lady? Hmmm, don't know if I like that if it's her, Mike."

"She's harmless," as I tried to deflect her comment and jealous demeanor.

"She's a knockout, isn't she?"

"Yeah, well, she looks nice." *That is an understatement I told myself. Something not right here, something is out of whack.*

The look on Katy's face just about said it all. I was beginning to believe my theory that she *was* jealous. Katy had been my friend through thick and thin. Did I give her the impression I was interested? I tried really hard to remain friends, just friends. I care a lot for Katy but could never see us together. She's young, most likely too young for me. Sure, I considered a relationship with her. I almost asked her out once, but all along I thought she was playing good ole, girl next door Katy. But, the look on her face right now was one that made me glad she wasn't carrying a weapon.

"Hey, Katy...Katy, dear!"

She snapped out of her mini-trance and just stared blankly. I wanted another drink. Suddenly, she gave me a half smile and asked if I would have another. I nodded my head, and then she smiled a big Katy O'Neal smile that I am used to.

She poured me another scotch, and I thanked her. She smiled and asked, "I'm still your favorite bartender, right?" she asked.

"There's not another one like you. Here's to you, Katy dear."

I raised my glass and finished a couple of sips and kept my eye on her, just to see if that look returned. It didn't, fortunately. I like my friends to stay friendly, the few that I have anyway. We continued to talk and visit, Katy with the gleaming eyes and me, with mostly nervous eyes, awaiting my date.

It was 6:55 and no sign of my date. Branch was going to make me wait, which I liked. At the stroke of seven, she made an entrance. I waved at her from the bar, and she immediately saw me. The manager and friend of mine, Nick, escorted her to my favorite table while I tipped Katy and told her if this didn't go well, I'd be back in an hour. She grinned and said, "I hope you have a nice evening." That totally shocked the hell out of me.

"Uh, oh... I, uh, will," I kind of stammered as I know I must have looked at her funny. My mind was not getting wrapped around Katy's mind set, and I was wondering why that bothered me. But soon, my mind became totally focused on the most gorgeous woman in the place. Ouch, a shot in the heart.

"Good evening, Ms. Branch. May I have the pleasure of dining with you?"

"Oh, but, of course, you know the pleasure is all mine," she said as smooth as silk.

"Then the gentleman will have a seat." Nick said as I stood there feeling in awe of this beauty.

"Hey, thanks, Nick. Nick, this is Allison Branch."

Nick reached out to shake her hand and held it a bit too long for my liking, but hey, she is a knockout as Katy suggested. Nick finally released her hand and said he would be right there with our server for the evening. As he turned to walk away he said to me "lucky" under his breath. But, he said it with a smile and was off to make our evening a good one.

Allison Branch was dressed for the occasion. Her dress was pearl colored, short; showing off her gorgeous legs... Her hair was falling around her shoulders. It was curled but not overly done. It flowed around her face, which was perfectly done with a soft light-red lipstick that was subtly suggestive. Her eyes of steel blue made me feel uncomfortable for some reason I couldn't put my finger on. Her smile was movie star white. I did not deserve this. Or did I?

"Good evening, Allison, great to see you again." I was wondering if my date would leave me after a quick rush to the ladies' room, but I think she was going to stay. "I must say you are stunning this evening"

"Funny, Mike, I have looked forward to this all day. You are as handsome as I imagined you to be tonight. Do you mind if I go freshen up in the ladies' room?"

Uh, oh.

"Just kidding, Mike, you know me."

Ah, much better, now I can relax. Just think I went from Brenda Jackson to Allison Branch. Yeah, Nick, I am lucky.

Nick returned to the table with a server in tow. We ordered drinks and started to talk, and strangely enough, not about the case. We were talking about our lives, our backgrounds. We talked about our siblings, parents, friends, and relatives. I had a scotch and Allison ordered wine, a merlot that just went right along with her appearance tonight.

I couldn't get away from the steel blue eyes that held mine as she talked on about how she made detective. Yeah, I forgot, it's Detective Allison Branch. I just goofily nodded, however, each word held my interest. I listened intently as Allison talked on and then we were about to get to the best part when she out of the blue opened up and said,

"Mike, do you believe in destiny?" I coughed on my scotch as I didn't even begin to know where that came from. "You know, like when you meet a guy and you really like him...a lot. You just know that meeting was meant to be. Do you believe in that, or not?"

"Well, I never do when I meet a guy."

"You know what I mean, Mike. Do you believe?"

"Well, that depends. Sometimes I do, but there always seems to be a black cloud that follows me around. It tends to rain on my destiny, at least it has before." *And just in the "Nick" of time the server and Nick re-appear. Hell, I was messing this up big time.*

"Would you both like another drink?" our server, who introduced himself as Kevin, asked.

"Of course, for me and Allison, for you?" She nodded and smiled. Kevin then put in the drink order and returned to take our dinner order. We both ordered. I peeked over my shoulder towards the bar area to see if Katy was still there to make my drink. I always wanted her to be there as she tended to make my scotch and waters just right. But, I saw that she wasn't which really seemed early to me for her to be gone.

Kevin arrived with our drinks and I returned to the destiny topic determined to make an "A" grade on this response. "Allison, I do believe in destiny, but I also believe you make your destiny happen. Sometimes destiny can't hold you because it came around at the wrong time. And other times destiny wins, because the relief pitcher comes into the game and seals the deal. It's timing, all a matter of timing."

"So, for you, it is timing and luck. For me it seems to be destiny. Therefore, no matter which, we're happy tonight in this setting, right?"

"Absolutely." We finished dinner and continued the conversation. Most of it was light and not too difficult. She teased me a few times, especially about not being able to fight well and protect myself. I had to laugh because she was right.

I asked for Nick one last time to tell him thanks and left Kevin a tip. We both agreed it was time to get out of there and move on to deeper discussions. We left her car there and headed to the Sidecar for a nightcap until I blurted, "Want to go someplace quiet?"

"Well, I thought you would never get around to asking," she said.

CHAPTER 18

We walked up the stairs to my condo and I actually felt comfortable, not nervous, just thinking of going in and continuing our dinner discussion. I couldn't help but flash back to the kick to the side of my head. I was trying to remember what I saw in the dark. It wasn't coming to me. I unlocked the door and set the alarm. Allison strolled to my couch while I suggested a nightcap. She nodded, and I went to the kitchen and poured a light Bailey's Irish Crème over ice into two glasses and returned.

We sipped through a light conversation. My gut talked too, telling me this woman was intriguing. I couldn't take my eyes from hers. They are like that. They pull you closer to her. She was talking about how she had enjoyed the evening and I couldn't help but feel that this night would be special. I could sense something happening. Those eyes...they hold you.

REDEMPTION

CHAPTER 19

I awoke to an empty bed. I must have slept hard, but my partner from the evening before was gone. The only trace of her was a good morning text.

"Had to get up and get to the station. Have a lead and thought I better get on it. Last night was beautiful. We must do that again soon. Hugs."

I answered, *"Yes, we must."*

And then, slowly I sat up on the bed remembering her fragrance, her softness, and her tears. Wow. That was something. Can I ever be a guy that has a relationship work? My whole life has been one up and down rollercoaster. When will it be on the straight stretch? I don't really deserve this.

The Saturday routine unfolds. Shower. Coffee. I had breakfast at the diner. I always enjoyed a fried breakfast at the Heartland Diner on Saturdays. I had nowhere else to go and usually no one else to do anything with. Shortly after the first sip of coffee, my ex-father-in-law called, asking to join me at the diner.

I felt funny knowing I had amazing sex with someone last night and now was going to talk to my late ex-wife's father. But, I still wanted to stay in touch and help them get through this.

Jerry arrived about fifteen minutes later. The waitress had yet to take my order. We said our pleasantries and began to talk about the case and what was going on. He was brief, and, for the first time, he seemed nervous, ill at ease.

"Jerry, I wish I had a better lead on who might have been stalking Sheila. I don't even know how I damn near got kicked to death in my own home. It happened so fast."

"Yeah, they must have been skilled. You just don't know who the hell you are dealing with anymore."

"Yeah, no shit. How's Margaret?" I asked.

"Not so good, Mike. She has nightmares and with this investigation going on with you now, she lays awake at night a lot. Man, I know she's hurting and I know she needs answers. Margaret will never accept Sheila's death unless she knows the truth. But, I'm not blaming you. Just wish we could have seen you guys together, grandkids and all."

I'm sorry, I truly am."

"Oh well, we have to keep moving on. I think Margaret needs some therapy sessions. She just can't accept what was going on," Jerry said.

We finally got our order and began to eat, mostly in silence. Some conversation about baseball and who was leading their divisions, who was getting traded this off-season, and who was going to win it this year.

When we finished, Jerry stood and said he needed to meet a friend.

"No need to rush off, I have always enjoyed your company."

"I know, but I got to run. Mike, keep us posted on

what is going on. We still fear for you and even us. I can't believe that things have escalated to this level. Someone is at the bottom of this, and we need to end this once and for all."

"Okay, Jerry, I'll keep in contact. Tell Margaret hello and I will get by to see her soon."

CHAPTER 20

Katy sat alone. Katy was crying. Katy was angry. Katy told Nick she wasn't feeling well and that she had to go home. But in reality, Katy was hurt, not sick. She wanted Mike and was more than pissed at this Detective Branch. So angry, that she was in tears.

Katy O'Neil had had a rough childhood. She had been neglected by her father after her mother was killed in a car accident when she was twelve. Her father did his best to raise her, but drank heavily after his wife died. Katy tried to help him but to no avail. By the time she had reached sixteen, she was pretty much on her own. Her older sister tried to help out but had three kids of her own to keep up with. Katy hit the streets at seventeen and partied hard. She experimented with marijuana and drank beer, but she managed to finish high school only because her sister kept track of her.

Katy moved out at eighteen and took a job as a

waitress at O'Shea's Restaurant until she turned twenty-four. She enrolled in community college and earned her associate's degree in graphic design. However, she struggled to find a job in the field. Every interview proved painfully challenging because she felt unsure of herself, always. She hated this relentless, irrational doubt; however, her self-recognition of this flaw only increased her insecurities. The tragic upbringing left her flat and alone. After many job rejections, she returned to O'Shea's because it was in her comfort zone—be nice, smile, and get tips. Katy got tips on her good looks alone. She lived in her own apartment complex and drove her own car, but not much else to show financially for her life up to this point.

Nick promoted her to bar manager and she seemed to take to the job naturally. She liked talking to people and listening to them. She did not like to tell her own story. She could talk to the drinkers on things they wanted to hear and she was street smart enough not to be taken advantage of. She was tough enough, but she had an extremely sensitive side that she did not want to reveal. She was pretty, very pretty.

I met Katy when she first started waiting tables at O'Shea's. She had a gleaming smile, beautifully tinted brunette hair and a very attractive figure. She was easy to like. I encouraged her to try interviewing for the graphic design jobs again, but she had been bitten and would not be bitten again. We became friends and many times I wished I had made a play for her. Possibly I could help her, but then again maybe not. As many people as I hurt in my life, maybe I would harm her. Once I asked Katy to my lake place to go hiking and just to enjoy the north woods. It was private but had no intentions on anything romantic. Just time to get out and enjoy something besides the city. We had fun and enjoyed drinks, but we slept in different rooms. Breakfast was made by Katy and conversation was slow. Was she disappointed that nothing happened? I took her back after breakfast as she had to go to work, but once again, another time it was...awkward.

Nevertheless, Katy was **MY** bartender and I wouldn't let anyone hurt her. How ironic is it that I was the one hurting Katy, and yet really had no idea I was doing so?

Katy wanted to punch something. She was so frustrated.

He looks at HER different than he looks at me! She is that gorgeous one with a cool job that impresses men like Mike. He's such a dumb ass. He could have me. I would treat him right. He would be so loved. God, I hate him. I hate HER. Why not me, Mike, why not me? More tears. Quit crying, you stupid baby. You're weak, Katy, so weak. Couldn't even stop the old man from drinking, ran away from it. Weak, weak! Well, then do something about it. Tell him off, tell her off, get him in bed and make him love you; he would love me in bed. I need him back and she needs to stay away from him. I want him. Bad. More tears. Weak...

CHAPTER 21

School was uneventful today but I was looking forward to another evening with Ms. Branch. She invited me to her place for a drink or two and some dinner. The night air was cool and snow was beginning to fall in the street by the time I drove up to her place. I knocked on the door and gave her a quick peck on the cheek as she took my coat, hat and gloves.

"I am glad you are here, Mike. I seem to have missed you more today than any other. I was so glad you were able to come by. I have prepared a nice roasted chicken and vegetable dinner I think you will like. The wine is chosen just for you, I think it will be to your liking."

"I am glad to be in such wonderful company, you look lovely. Your hair looks great and you smell sweet. I am a lucky man tonight!"

She brought back two wineglasses and a bottle of white. We each had a glass and tapped them together in recognition of the evening together.

"Mike, I am having fun being with you. You seem to fill a void in my life. I was not sure at first what it would come to, if anything, but I am feeling more and more comfortable with you. Could it be my destiny or like you say, just my good luck?"

"Maybe both," I responded.

We sipped our wine sitting close together on the couch. She set hers down and leaned the side of her head against my shoulder. It felt as though the weight of things that were bothering her were being laid upon my chest. She looked up at me with her bright blue eyes and seemed to be asking me to kiss her. I leaned towards her and began to press my lips to hers...

Her phone rang loud, disturbing my thoughts and the fantasy world that I was hoping to make, I was brought back to real time.

"This is Branch...yeah...hmm... okay, Marx, I'll meet you in about ten minutes."

"Work?" I asked.

"Yeah, Marx, needs me to come to the station and follow up on a lead on the other case we are working on. I need to get down there. Sorry, Mike, this will have to wait, but don't leave, I will be back soon."

She presses two fingers to her lips and then places them on my cheek. It was her job I know, but why right now? This was becoming magical and I didn't want to snap back and forth from fantasy to reality.

"I know, but do hurry back, we have unfinished business and an unfinished bottle of wine," I replied. "That would mean on the double."

I watched her leave and then focused my attention to the snow outside. It was falling heavier than when I first came here and I thought that maybe a short walk in the snow would help me think and try to decide if this was a person I could be with. I put on my coat and gloves and made my way outside. I left the door unlocked as I didn't have a key, but felt safe enough in this neighborhood. The first few steps into the empty street would only leave shallow footprints as the snow was not too heavy yet.

I walked with my head down as I watched my feet making prints in the snow. The streetlights were on and it reflected on the flakes that were becoming much larger.

Is this someone for me? Do I really know her? What is she about? My mind was racing with the possibilities. Something gave me pause, something that she said before. I couldn't quite draw on what it meant so I let it go.

I passed a few trash dumpsters on her parking lot and thought I had heard a noise. I turned to look but found nothing there. I went along with my walk and had a funny feeling that I should walk faster. No real reason for it but I started to pick up my pace. It was getting colder anyway so I could get back and wait for Allison. Just as suddenly and just like before, I felt a crashing thud on my head and once again my world was black.

CHAPTER 22

I came to with an incredibly searing pain in my head and eyes. I tasted and felt blood on the left side of my face. There wasn't much light and it made me think at first that I was partially blind.

Where was I? What is happening to me? I instantly began to think that someone wanted me dead. I felt my hands unable to move. My feet, what about my feet? No luck as I realized that I was tied up and there was no light where I could see what to do next. Okay, I was in a chair, I could feel that and figure that out. I've been kidnapped. I was sure I was being stowed away in some place that no one would ever find. So many questions. Who hit me, who took me and where in the hell was I? I was afraid to yell out as someone there would hit me again. I was sure I was concussed as the headache was almost unbearable. I could make out a small light, very faint and hardly discernible. But there was no way to figure where I was and how I was going to escape this mess.

I was groggy and unable to form words. I tried to talk out loud but nothing was coming out. I needed to get out of this predicament, but I had no contact with anyone. No one is going to hear me if I yell. Is there someone else here, waiting and watching and if I make a false move, will I be in darkness again? This is incredible. A teacher, former prosecutor being held by people he did not know and for reasons that seemed uncertain. I thought that maybe it was this stalker, this person that had scared Sheila. Of course, it had to be that right? I felt a sharp pain in my right arm and suddenly was grabbed by a hand to hold me still. I became much sleepier and I could not resist and once again darkness, my new friend, took me for a ride.

CHAPTER 23

Branch returned to her apartment and found no sign of Mike. She immediately went to check to see if his car was still there. It was parked in the exact same spot. No footprints in the snow near his car and no footprints in the snow on the sidewalk. The snow was now falling at a terrific rate and there probably were no footprints anywhere. Branch began searching the apartment frantically, as she looked for something, something that would verify this situation. She found what she was looking for on her kitchen table. It was written in orange lipstick and stated, "We Have Him."

Allison stared at the note and then quickly folded it and placed it in her handbag. She dialed Marx and he answered on the first ring.

"Hello, Marx here. What's up, Branch?"

"Funny deal here. When you called me to come to the station, I left Parsons here to wait for me. I came back and he is gone. His car is still in the parking lot.

No sign of forced entry. It's like he walked right out of here and disappeared," she said.

"That's pretty odd, but why not just get in his car and leave if he got tired of waiting on you?" Andy said.

"Yeah, it doesn't make sense. I know he likes to go to O'Shea's for drinks and has a bartender friend there named Katy. Why don't you go and check her out and ask her a few questions?"

"You have seen the snow, right?"

"Yes, I know, but this is important."

"Okay, okay, I'll go on over. But maybe he has another girl and just dumped you. You know the guy's past, right? He may have just gotten a ride out of your life," Marx said sarcastically. "But I will go over there."

"Thanks, Marx, I owe you one." *Yes, I do know his past Marx. Asshole.*

Marx hung up and Allison bit her lip. *What to do next. This is becoming much tougher than she thought. Okay, just be calm and don't get excited. Get yourself together and quit falling apart like you always do. Use your head and think, THINK DAMN IT!*

CHAPTER 24

*B*ack to consciousness, I was feeling sick. My vision was blurred and nothing was still. I could feel myself spinning in circles and laughing inside my head. I have realized that I am being drugged. By whom? My mind is racing but my thoughts are coming to me in slow motion. Wake up! I just didn't feel that I was alive. I kept telling myself that I was dead, that my visions were only coming from either heaven or hell. Where was I? This was my payment for all I have done wrong. Stuck here for eternity, never again to have another coherent thought. I saw James fishing with me in the boat. I saw Katy pouring me a drink and giving me a slurred statement. I saw Sheila and her pasty face in the casket. Wake up! These images are not real and I was seeing them from above them. Somebody... save me...

James was curious as Mike did not call and was late

for their breakfast get together. He called twice and there was no answer. He called upstairs to Monica and told her he was going by Mike's place just to check him out.

James arrived at Mike's condo about 9:00 am. He did not see Mike's car in the parking lot, but there were times before that Mike got another ride home. He went to the door and rang the doorbell twice. There was no answer. *Okay, brother, where were you?* Something in James' gut was saying to him that something was way out of sync here. No matter how late Mike stayed out, he never stood him up for breakfast. He thought of calling the police but he was jumping the gun, he thought. Okay, I'm not going to be the guy that didn't report it. He only had one more place to look before he panicked. He was going to drive out to the lake house to see if Mike went there for the weekend.

James started on the twenty-mile trip and was thinking of how irresponsible Mike used to be. But he knew he was more settled now, but he was always taken by spur of the moment thinking. Mike was funny that way. Especially after the divorce. *Ah shit, I'll just turn around. He's probably with that detective somewhere.* So, James turned his Expedition around and headed home to Monica.

WAKE UP!! Someone there? Someone was yelling at me cursing me. "Wake up you, son of a bitch!" My eyes open slightly and the brightest light shone into the two small slits that were my eyes. "You, asshole, this is what you get. Everything was your fault."

Nothing about the voice was familiar, a voice I had never heard before. Strangely low pitched but definitely a female. My eyes were starting to focus and what was in front of me was dressed in a black hood and ball cap, that much I could see. But the face, it was black, no, it was masked. It was time to be fearful as I could quickly feel my throat burn with dryness. I needed water, something, I could not speak. I tried to form the words 'water' with my lips.

'Water?' she laughed. You're not getting any water! I hope you die here. But before you do, I am going to make you pay. You are going to pay for what you did to Sheila!" she screamed.

"Whoooo arrr yooooo?" my voice cracked and creaked. It wasn't me saying that was it? That couldn't be my voice. Everything so slow, not real.

"You'll find out soon enough, asshole. Soon enough," The Voice replied.

With that, a hard blow to the rib cage took all my breath away. I winced with pain and hung my head, trying to catch any remaining breath I could muster. I wanted to yell out and curse them, I could not form the words. I was drifting again, drifting, drifting...darkness.

In the darkness there were people I knew. This was a party, right? C'mon man, wake up! At the party were the people I worked with as a prosecutor. Drinks were flowing and the ridicule was painful. Patty, my legal assistant, my assistant PA Bob Duncan, other attorneys were there, people I beat in court in previous trials. Everyone was laughing and pointing at me.

"You know he lost his license, don't you?"

Such a fool, that guy, drank himself out of the job.

"Started losing cases," the accusatory finger pointing at me as they kept laughing.

Laughing, loudly hideously, they kept punishing me with their comments. I tried to leave, but I couldn't get out of my chair. My body was motionless and lifeless.

"What an asshole," they said. "Had the world by the tail but couldn't quit the drinking, carousing, staying out late.

I must be in hell...

CHAPTER 25

A ndy Marx was smart. Tops in his class at the police academy. He was also good looking and could have his pick of anyone. He was tall at 6' 2" and sleek and fit. His current partner in the class, Allison Branch, finished second. She didn't like to lose to anyone. Andy tolerated Allison. He thought her to be a spoiled brat and topping her at the academy was quite pleasurable. Branch didn't really want Andy as a partner, but he was rising quickly on the force and she could envision him passing her again. Andy was raised Catholic and had five siblings. He worked hard to get where he was on the force and he intended to go farther. He always had goals and, in his mind, he could see no one keeping him from achieving those goals.

He walked into O'Shea's and headed for the bar. He intended to question Katy but he thought he needed to notify the owner first. He found Nick and flashed his badge.

"Looking for Katy O'Neal. I have a few questions I'd like to ask her," Andy said.

"She's working but let me get someone to watch her shift while you talk. You can use my office," Nick replied.

Nick sent a young man to replace Katy and then showed Andy and Katy to his office. Andy sat down in one of the chairs opposite Nick's desk and Katy remained standing.

Nick introduced Andy as Detective Marx from the Milwaukee PD. They shook hands briefly and then Katy sat in the chair by the water cooler. Katy seemed really nervous, as if she had seen the police before, bringing her bad news.

"What's this about," she said rubbing her hands together nervously. She looked away from him hoping he would just go away, but she knew that wouldn't happen.

"How well do you know a Mr. Mike Parsons?" he began.

"Really well. We are good friends and he comes in often to see m... I mean to have a drink," she replied.

"Do you know he is missing? He was at the apartment of my partner, Detective Branch, and she had to be called out yesterday. He must have left but never returned. Seems that he is not around. He could be many places I assume. Branch tried to call his cell, but there is no answer. In fact, GPS can't trace it, either."

Katy's hand was over her mouth, in surprise, she could not answer immediately. *Oh no, what has happened?* She was in shock, but yet knew she must answer.

"I haven't seen him for a few days. He and I are good friends. *But for me, it is more than that.* We see each other here at the bar at least once a week sometimes two nights. "

Katy was thinking and slowing down, being careful. She didn't want this guy to know what she and Mike were investigating. *Mike had his reasons and I have his back.*

"Would you say he drinks a lot?"

"Not especially, comes in for a scotch or two and leaves. We always talk and have good conversations. Nothing more than that."

"You do know that he is in a relationship with my partner? That he is now nowhere to be found and that his car was left where he parked it. In my mind, he may be missing but possibly worse. Anything you can tell me about this would be helpful."

Katy wanted to blurt out that she was quite jealous of his partner, Detective Branch. She wanted to tell him to find him and that she had more than a passing interest in Mike. Reasoning told her that she then would become a person of interest.

"Well, there isn't much more to tell. We are friends, but I, too, am concerned about his being missing. But, really, I don't think I can help much more."

"Well, if you think of something that would help, here's my card. Give me a call."

Marx then shook hands with Katy and left the room.

Katy was worried. *I do have a thing for Mike and I am insanely jealous of the pretty detective. She caused this, if not for her, Mike would be safe and not in danger. Maybe he is safe and not in danger. But he is a person who follows routine and since he hasn't been here, I need to check it out. Why hadn't he picked her? She would have given him a safe place to be. With me. I could have helped him, taken care of him. Loved him...*

Nick appeared and was concerned by the look on

Katy's face. She seemed distant and very far away. He had been good to Katy and treated her like one of his own daughters.

"Katy, Katy...hey you okay? Do you want the rest of the night off or can you stay? It will be okay if you go this time, maybe it can give you time to pull things together." *Nick said with a genuine concern*

"Sure, Nick, I think I will go. I'll get some rest and be back tomorrow. I have some things I need to sort out. I think Mike may be in trouble." Katy replied, the far away stare still in her eyes...

"Okay, but kid don't get involved in this and don't do anything stupid. Let the authorities handle it."

Katy drove home and in the midst of her drive, she thought once more about why she couldn't have what she wanted. It would have all been better had Mike just picked her instead of that detective. She would have made his life better. He would have been loved, needed, respected. She would find him. She just had to.

CHAPTER 26

J erry and Margaret were beginning to see the problems that death in a family especially that of their child, could bring. Beginning to rear its ugly head was blame, anger, and indifference. Jerry had become more hostile in his speech, preferring to belittle and talk down to his wife. Margaret had become reticent and was dismissing herself from reality. She began to take medications to escape her grief. Jerry had tried to have her make it through her mourning without it. But she had gotten worse and he relented to the doctors' advice and recommendations. Their marriage, that always seemed to have a hint of domination to it, was quickly disintegrating to ashes.

The business was going south and Jerry needed an infusion of cash as a way to save the business he had spent his entire life building. He had some contacts that could help make this happen. The problem was that the contacts were shady and underhanded, which could cause him a multitude of problems. He decided that even so, dealing with these people was the easiest way to get out of the hole.

Jerry was a strong man, with an intense desire to succeed. He would not let this business fail. Sheila's death had almost derailed him from that success. In a sick way, even Jerry would not be stopped by that, much to the dismay of his catatonic wife. He pushed on, working long hours, and, yet, he was going nowhere. He had to find a way.

Jerry's phone rang and he picked it up on the second ring.

"Hello."

"I need to meet you as soon as possible. Something has come up that you need to know about," the Voice replied.

"Where and when? I have some things to get done here so I can't drive too far," Jerry said.

"No problem, just drive to the Sidecar and we can talk. The news is interesting and I am sure that your new-found cash infusion will be worth it. The delivery and the supplier are now in sight. I'll tell you more when you get there, just don't want to say anything else..."

"Look, just you this time, don't bring those others. I am dealing with you and you alone on this thing. We made a deal and that deal just may be what I need to get my business and my emotional life back on track. Too many people involved will surely mess it up."

"Okay, just me and you," the Voice replied.

As Jerry rubbed his forehead trying to shake from his head what he was getting involved in, "I'll be there shortly."

Jerry hung up and began to feel that pounding in his head he felt for the last month. The headaches had started to make him sick, but he had things to do. He had to get his business back and his daughter's death had taken so much from him. He needed to square the deal and someone was going to pay.

At the Sidecar, the Voice was nervous as it waited for Jerry to arrive. The Voice needed a drink. The Voice needed more than that actually. The Voice needed a serious hit. The plan was all along about friends, money and being able to crawl out from under the poverty known as a child. This guy, Jerry, had the cash to make it go, and he had the will to see it through. But the Voice did not trust Jerry. He was older and didn't understand this new generation. We will be dominant in the future and guys like him will disappear. We can use him and then dispose of him. That's what was in the Voice's head. Disposable people, after all, are what the new generation was all about, right?

The Voice spotted Jerry and waved the friendly wave that only an assassin could. Bring them in and then BAM! Use them, and then destroy them.

Jerry sat down in the booth across from the Voice. His features were looking more worn by the day. And the headaches, ah the headaches. He had a doctor's appointment tomorrow, but for now he needed this meeting so he was trying to shake it off.

"Look, the plan is now into place. Fifty grand invested in the drug market, making us players in a much bigger world. Profits will double and triple in three months. Your wishes have been met and now it is time to follow through with the rest of the plan." The Voice said in a low tone.

"Okay, I'm in. But you know there are two parts to my request to meet all conditions. How am I assured that part two gets done?" Jerry said as he folded his hands and placed them on the table in front of him. He was assessing the Voice and was trying to read "double-cross" or "bullshit in the Voice's face.

"Look, I told you part two will get done. Much of what you anticipated is already in the works. For your information, the player you needed is now available."

Jerry looked over the Voice's head distantly. "It's more important than the cash that part two takes place. You know where I am on that. I have connections and you know that. You slip up, and you'll be at the bottom of Lake Michigan."

The Voice was not moved. The stoic expression said all that Jerry needed to hear. "Not worried at all. This has gone well and I expect it to make you the cash you need. The players are private and very rich... They are going to make you, me, all of us rich. You got to trust me on this."

Jerry smiled and looked directly into the eyes of the Voice. "Just remember, I've got nothing to lose. All of it is a gamble. That makes me a dangerous guy." Jerry knew he didn't trust the Voice and he was already thinking of a good way to take care of this loose cannon.

"Sure, Jerry, sure. Look it's all good. No need to worry, but part two is officially a go."

Jerry finished his scotch and was ready to leave, satisfied that he was assured of everything. He dropped a twenty on the table and walked off from the Voice. The Voice looked at him leave and thought *"easy to take down. Such an ego...easy to take down."*

Jerry got in his Mercedes and began to drive back to his office. He needed another drink and a pill, maybe two. He was in it deep and there was no turning back. He thought of his father and everything the old man taught him about business. He felt a failure, and now he just had to get it back. This is the only way. Failure in business was not an option, and he was going to succeed. He had to.

Branch was in a hurry. Mike's brother, James, had called Marx and explained how unusual Mike's disappearance was. Marx told him the car would be impounded and dusted for prints. Branch was sure that since the car was locked that there would be none, but Marx wanted to follow through anyway.

Branch needed to know where Mike was being held. She needed to find out quickly. Marx's police chatter was taking up her time. She was paranoid. Once again, that idiot Marx, was trying to upstage her. Mr. First in the Class was beginning to piss her off. She hung up and said she would meet Marx later and they could go over the existing information. Marx had doubts about Branch as a partner, but he was a team player and a hustler, so comparing notes was fine with him. He knew he would break this case before she did. She had too much doubt, too much self-loathing, yet, the police sense, Andy had. She knew it, too, and she would do anything to be first in the class this time. Andy Marx was not getting her promotion. Andy Marx would also not find Mike first. She was going to make sure of that.

CHAPTER 27

B reanne Jackson was the wayward sister of Brenda Jackson. Their mother had always said that Breanne was wild and needed guidance. She fought in school, physically and verbally with other girls and sometimes boys. She had very few friends and her sister Brenda, was mostly embarrassed by her.

Breanne was a regional martial art fighting champion. She had found this through her school counselor who had taken an interest in helping her find a release for her anger. She referred Breanne to her friend, an instructor at the downtown martial arts academy. Breanne was only twelve at the time but she learned quickly and was quite athletic, although school sports were not her thing. Her "thing" was hanging with the stoners in school and defying her teachers, her mother, and, most importantly, her sister.

Once at school, Breanne was smoking pot in the

restroom her junior year. A snitch saw her and turned her in to the principal. She was suspended from school and had to repeat her junior year, much to the dismay of her mother. The snitch was walking home and Breanne beat her senseless. This caused her to be detained at the juvenile center and that was the beginning of some run-ins with the law.

She graduated on the five-year plan, although her mother thought it would never happen and began hanging out with the same old friends again. A few more scrapes with the law later, Breanne was given the choice of jail or finding a job. She kept training all the while and her instructor kept her as a pupil, although he was hesitant to do so.

Breanne was employed by a local company as an errand girl in the office mail room. She learned a bit of social grace there, and her junior high counselor kept tabs on her. She was also winning martial arts tournaments. She worked out incessantly and was developing into a state and national contender. She was getting her share of attention from the men at the office, but her interest was not in the opposite sex. Ever since junior high, she realized her feelings were for the same sex. She was gay and she knew it. She also knew her sister was gay and was hanging some with Brenda and her friends. Although Brenda tried hard to include Breanne, it always turned sour on her during most of those occasions. The biggest reason Brenda tried to help Breanne, was she told her mother who raised them by herself, that she would try and keep an eye on her. When Breanne started to receive more attention from Brenda's friends, Brenda became a bit more distant from her sister. Preferring smaller gatherings to group nights out, Brenda was getting out of the loop. Her only friend, from high school, was Sheila Linhart-Parsons, soon to be Sheila Linhart again as she was getting divorced from her insufferable husband, Mike.

Sheila and Brenda struck up their old friendship easily. They began to have smaller gatherings with their friends and sometimes the two of them would go take in movie together. Brenda wanted more of a relationship and Sheila discussed this with her but was unsure of what she wanted. Sheila wanted to be loved. She pondered and considered this. But she couldn't make up her mind. Breanne knew Sheila as her sister's friend. Sheila had always treated Breanne well. She was always nice to her and defended her to Brenda, which Breanne really liked. But once again, as Breanne began to flirt with Sheila at some of the get togethers, Sheila was not as affectionate towards her as Breanne would have wanted. As always, there was an awkward blow up initiated by Breanne.

Brenda and Breanne shared the same martial arts trainer, Jared Simms. Brenda had been passed by Breanne a few years before, and she no longer was the favored pupil. For this reason, Brenda quit going to the downtown academy. Breanne was the new star in town. Brenda moved on, but was not quite willing to forgive her baby sister for passing her up in the martial arts ranks. Nor was she very inclusive with her circle of friends. Call it sibling rivalry or just a normal family falling out, but the two were becoming more distant each year.

Breanne was short at 5'4" but powerfully built. She had no fat percentage to speak of. In fact, she was the more attractive of the two sisters. Brenda also knew this and it also, of course, upset her. In fact, there were a lot of things that upset her about Breanne. It was always the squeaky wheel getting the grease. She had her mother's attention, Sheila's attention, and their trainer's attention. When would this stop? As long as her mother was alive, she had promised to look after Breanne. She would do that because she loved her mother.

There was something wrong with Breanne these days, and Brenda was going to find out. She had to be seeing someone, and that someone had some influence in her behavior. She would look into it. Little sister had something going on and Brenda was not above snooping to find out.

CHAPTER 28

I am surviving but I don't know how. Once again, my sight is blurry. My body is cold and I need something. My mind is saying a drink, yes alcohol. My dream is fading and my mind is fuzzy but I knew who I am. I knew I am in danger, as my condition is still serious. I could hurl and there was nowhere to hurl but here. Nowhere to go, I wasn't walking anywhere.

Where is the redemption I seek? I am going to die here. Meet my Karma here. This is how it ends? Every man wants to have redeeming qualities. It doesn't matter who else is proud of you. It matters if you are proud of yourself. My qualities were not good enough. No way to redeem me, no way that others see me how I want them to see me. I couldn't communicate, I couldn't express myself. Everyone said he's just a quiet man. But I was a stifled man. Too afraid to speak my mind and let people know what I wanted. What I needed. How I felt. Thinking *that my thoughts, my inner feelings really mattered to no one but myself.*

A hideous man living this hideous life. Reaching, groping for a handle on what I should be, what I could be. Branch is not here. She probably thinks I left her. Being the same ole Mike again. But I know what is happening here. I am a target for murder. These people are going to kill me. Is it Brenda? Her friends? Is it the people who stalked Sheila, the same people who wrote on my door and sent me the letter? Someone has to help me out of this.

The light switched on and it shone directly into my face. Blinded immediately by the harsh glare of a laser, the light went directly to my pupils. Cringing from the light, I squinted to try and make out the figures. Three were staring at me through eyeholes in their masks. They had coats with hoods and wore boots. The taller one spoke first and with a quiet voice began.

"You are here for a reason. It appears that quite probably that reason is that you drove your ex-wife to suicide. It is my understanding that you made her feel alone and alienated. You drank and stayed out late. You ignored her. She was our friend, and what she told us about you, was horrible. You must have no feelings, no understanding of the feelings of others. Obviously, you must be a huge prick."

"Sheila had her own problems and she alienated me," I said through puffy lips. "I don't even know who you are, so why do I have any need to respond to this?"

The silhouette inched closer and I could smell its breath. It reeked of beer and marijuana smoke.

"You, being the giant prick that you are, you are going down. You are going to die, but it will be slow. You will die in the way your Sheila did, with a drug overdose. It's simple really. People like you should be eliminated. You are a menace to the people that cross your path," it said with spittle coming from the mouth hole in its facemask.

I was silent and unable to respond. The voice was escalating to almost piercing degree. I was in deep trouble here and I was going to die. Plain and simple this is what my maker must have intended for me as punishment for having dubious character.

"Thump him," it said. With that, the smallest one kicked me on the outside of my knee. The pain was excruciating and I was sure my knee was snapped. It burned and the pain shot all the way down to my ankle. I thought I was going to darkness again, as white-hot spots were appearing before my eyes. The little one shrieked with glee from her assault. I thought it was crazy and could only think this must be a dream. It's not real, surely not real I kept telling myself. The end is near and this will not take long as I keep absorbing these blows.

"That's enough," the male said. "Keep him alive. It's in the plan."

"I know I could kill him. Let me have one more shot," she begged as I could see her body coiled and ready to strike again.

That voice, low and scratchy, I know that voice. Yes, the first one I saw, not wanting to give me water. I've heard it before but when? How? I know her, I know I know her...

"Let it go," the male said and turned away from me. "There is much more to do."

"You know you won't get away with this. They will find you. Even if you kill me, you will all be in jail," I gasped as I once again struggled for air.

"If you're dead, it doesn't really matter now, does it?"

The sense of impending doom filled my mind. They were right. If I was dead and no one found me, it would never really matter, would it? They were going to get away with it; they were going to get away with murder.

They left the room and turned off the light as I followed their footsteps, watching their angry gait go out into the cold. I felt the draft of the icy, outside air as they left and, to my shock and surprise, I saw briefly in the daylight of the door opening what looked like familiar landscape. I know it, I have been here before. Like a picture, like a dream, something so familiar. The clue to where I am is there.

I thought hard through the pain trying to recall this place, but just when I thought it was coming to me, the needle shot into my arm again, the third person there drilled me once again with another hit. Gently, I felt once again my old friend on my heels. My friend, the dark.

CHAPTER 29

Katy was worried. The man she so desperately needed was in trouble and she knew a name. She didn't give it to Marx and she hoped like hell she didn't need to give it to Branch. She didn't want to talk to Branch. Ever. She knew James, and thought to call him, but she was sure he would go right to Marx or worse yet, to Branch.

Katy had trouble finding what to wear. Most of her outfits she chose for Mike, when she knew it was a day that he might be there. Today she knew he would not be there. She had no desire to choose. This had to get solved. The one person, who could ever make her day, was missing. She had to find him. Maybe he was just skipping town for a few days, but she knew him better. He was a creature of habit, one who liked his routine.

Where to look? These people that he was messing with, had to be the ones who may have known about the stalking of Sheila. They were dangerous and she thought he was definitely in serious trouble. Her life was just one bad decision after another. She had to act. So, she picked up her phone and began to dial Nick. She would tell him that she couldn't come in today. That she was ill. But with that thought, she put the phone back down.

What's wrong with you? It is the weakness, this indecision that is defining your life. You know what your mind and even your heart is telling you to do. But, you can't go through with it. You are afraid to fail, afraid to act. This is what you have always been. Scared. A chicken, someone who freezes up. You pick up that phone and call Nick. Quit being so weak, isn't that what you have always been? Weak?

Katy picked up the phone and called.

"Hey Nick, this is Katy. Could you have Trish work for me today? I'm kind of feeling under the weather."

"Yeah, sure," Nick replied with a hint of suspicion in his voice. "I'm sure I can, but you want me to send one of the girls over to check on you?"

"No, I will be okay. I'm sure it will pass," she lied. She knew that she herself could be in jeopardy, but she had to do this. Just this once, she had to not be weak.

"Alright, I'll call Trish. I'm sure she'll help you out. I'm just worried about you."

"Look, Nick, I'm just as little sick that's all."

"Alright, get some rest and I'll see you tomorrow."

Katy hung up and bit her lip. She was surer than ever, that she had to do something. She had to help Mike. In the end, it will all be better. I find him and I will surely be with him. She dressed quickly in jeans and a sweater, finding her boots and parka. Gloves will be necessary too. If Nick calls again, I will say I was at the doctor's office. Katy turned off her location on her phone and began her journey to find Mike. She had no idea of what was going to happen. She had no idea what was in store for her... no idea.

—▲—

James dialed Detective Branch and was looking for help. He had waited to see if Mike might resurface but a couple days are alarming.

"This is Detective Branch. How can I help you?"

This is Mike's brother, James. I'm calling because I knew you and he were seeing each other. I'm really worried and I was hoping you might know something. It is really unusual for him to just leave like this."

"I'm worried too, James. I am working really hard and overtime to get some things done. I just don't have any clues." she said almost sobbing. "If you know anything, please call me and let me know. We were starting to get close, and I, too, am very worried. Give me your number and I will call if we know anything."

"When was he with you last?" James asked. "He was supposed to play golf with me two days ago. He never showed."

"Three nights ago, he came over for a drink and I got called out on a case, "Branch said. "I had no idea he would not be there when I got back. I know this is trying for you and it is for me, too. Be assured that we are going to do whatever it takes to find him," she said as she sounded almost tearful.

"I know that you will. Please keep in touch." James hung up and was contemplating that call. Something did not fit, something out of place. It was just a hunch, but he wanted to find out more.

James dialed Andy Marx's number but it went to voicemail. "This is James Parsons, Mike's brother. Please give me a call on this number. I think something is out of place and we need to talk."

Katy made the drive to Mike's lake cabin in forty minutes. She had been there before and knew the way. She parked and turned off the ignition and walked up the snowy walkway to the front door. Peeking through the side glass of the door, she tried to find some movement of some light that would let her know he was there. Not seeing his vehicle did not deter her as she was thinking something was sinister about this whole situation. The door was locked when she tried to open it. Katy decided to go around to the back and check. Maybe he left a door open.

Her feet sunk into the four inches of snow as she made her way carefully to the back of the cabin. She stopped abruptly as she was sure had heard something move in the nearby woods. She saw nothing but the stack of firewood and the out building about 100 yards away. No movement or sound.

Maybe I shouldn't be here. I just have to know, I have got to find him.

She walked a bit slower and listened intently for more noise, but the only thing she could hear was the crunching snow beneath her feet... Katy walked up the four steps of the screened-in back porch and opened the screen door. The door creaked slightly, causing her pulse to quicken, but she quickly went to check the back door and to her surprise it opened.

She looked around as she slowly moved around looking for some sort of clue that Mike had recently been there.

I was here. I had my chance and like always I blew it. I was weak. I've always been weak though, haven't I? Never could pull the old proverbial trigger, could you girl? Always waiting and anticipating. What was I afraid of? He was handsome, caring and kind. What was I waiting for......? Not opening up, just waiting for him to show that he cared. Waited too long...waited too long......

Katy turned and looked into the bedroom. Everything was neat and put away. It was just the way she remembered seeing it last. She turned away and felt that there was nothing here that could help her. She thought she had better lock the back door before leaving and began to head through the kitchen toward the back porch.

She never saw it coming as both figures jumped her from behind and as quickly as she opened her mouth to scream, one of them kicked her in the side of the face. Katy saw nothing else but darkness. Her nightmare was beginning.

CHAPTER 30

I could barely open my eyes. I was back into a dream. It was Friday night and it was pre-game. We had just finished putting all of our pads together. Forty other guys and I were getting ready for our rival football game. We knew the routine, everything on except shoulder pads and helmets. Heat balm smell, sugar tablets, and butterflies flying around in your stomach were all happening before the game.

This game was everything. It was for the conference championship and the chance to move into state play. We lay silent on the gym floor, staring directly into the ceiling. No talking was allowed as each man had to think of the jobs they had to do to execute the game plan. It was 6:45 and time for pre-game warm-ups. Silently, we fell in line and were ready for battle.

We left the locker room and the stadium was packed. We came in as always from the south side of the field to the roaring crowd and the band playing our fight song. Players, pumped and excited, ran to their specific position groups to warm-up. We needed this win. We had to have it. This is the win we have worked for all year.

During the first quarter of the game, we moved downfield at will, ten to fifteen yards at a clip. Our team was in red and black and theirs in all white. First and goal at their one-yard line. Our halfback gets the hand off and drives hard for the goal line. Yells, screams, cheers and...chaos. The ball is on the ground, no, no, no...fumbled? They recover. Silence.

They drive back on us. Down to midfield they go, running the ball hard and efficient. I was playing outside linebacker, and they kept sending three guys of the sweep to block. Our defensive end, Eric Tapper, wasn't taking out the blockers and they were gaining too many yards. In the defensive huddle I told Tapp, hey, you got to help me out. Take some of them out so we have a chance, you're killing me Tapp, just do it, you're killing me!...

"You're killing me, you're killing me," I was saying over and over realizing that I was opening my eyes again.

"Yes, we are going to do just that. But first we brought you a little present. We thought you may be getting too lonely here all day by yourself. We brought you this nosy little bitch to talk to while we make our plans to kill you. Not only you, but her, too. She got in the way, but she has to go, too."

There right before me, as I squinted to see what and who they were talking about, was my bartender, Katy. A dream? No, this was real. Her face was bloodied and bruised as they shone the light in our faces. Groggy and still limp, they tied her to a second chair. Both prisoners of some wild and crazy people, who had mayhem on their minds. I shouldn't have involved her. I think I know who one of these three is. But I had to take this slow. Don't piss them off too much yet. They would surely kill us.

Katy then took her first needle hit to la la land. They didn't bother with me. I had plenty in me and, for the pain, I was craving another.

They are going to kill us and overdose us, or just pump us so full of drugs that we could never get out or defend ourselves. My nightmare has turned into our nightmare. Katy and I stuck here, left to die here, wherever here was. I've got to be alert, figure this out. But the drugs are making this impossible to sort out reality from fantasy and dreams. I'm cold and sick, I need food, water and I need a hit.

The three walked out, and again, I peered to look at the opening and try to focus on what I could see in here. Anything that would give us a chance when they were gone. A few more days and it would be over. We had to get out of here.

Wake up Katy. Do something, take one of them out and give me a chance. You're killing me, Katy, wake up!!

Our eyes met as we both returned to consciousness. Her eyes met mine with a blank and disoriented stare. We are captive, both of us. Captive to whom? For what reason? I am beginning to find that black cloud kind of reasoning in my soul. It is my punishment for Sheila's death, and I was about to pay the highest price. If we didn't get out they would kill us both. My mouth was incredibly dry and too many more needles and I would be gone. I could not stay here and we just had to get out. Be tough, survive, and, yes, survive.

"Katy, can you hear me?"

"Yes, what's going on here?" she asked as her voice was weak and faint in the semi-darkness.

"Look, we have to find the way out of here. We can't just give up and become drug overdose victims. You know that is how they will make it look. The addictive ex-prosecutor and his girlfriend overdosing. They won't have to get rid of the bodies. Just untie us and let us lay here on this cold floor or even drag us somewhere else. The police will find us and then call it drug related. Our captives leave needles and pills around us. No way they get caught. So, look, let's decide right now we are going to survive. Every waking moment you have when they are here, you have to try and see what you can, feel what you can, and look for the way out. We don't have much time."

"Mike, I feel sick, tired and don't know if I can do this. You know me. I am just a weak person." she replied in a thick, slurred voice.

I knew Katy and I knew she had weaknesses in her ability to survive hardship I needed her to be on target and do what she could. I needed her to fight.

"Katy, listen to me. You can do this. I need you now more than ever. You have to think as hard as you can. You have to try to remain as alert as you can. They are drugging us and the time between needles is becoming less and less. It's now or never girl. We both have to fight."

"I need you now more than ever" is what Katy heard.

Yes, you do need me, I knew it all along. Why couldn't you tell me that before? I would have been there for you. Okay, for you, because I know more than anything, I need him. I will do this, I will fight.

"Okay, Mike, I will fight for you," she whispered with a tone of affection.

"Fight for us," I replied. "Fight for yourself, too. Just know if something happens to me, you need to fight for yourself. It's not just about me."

"You know I was in your lake house looking for clues to find you and hoping that you might be there. I walked around your place entering through the back door that was unlocked. I was kicked hard, and that is the last thing I remember."

I immediately knew where we were. If she was on this property more than likely they had found my outbuilding with the storm shelter. We were in my storm shelter, on the floor of the metal building I used for a workshop.

"Katy, I know where we are. We are in my storm shelter under the workshop. I am sure where we are."

"Mike, they will be back. They are going to put those needles in our arms again and we will be helpless," she said her voice again showing weakness and fear.

"One more time, Katy, I need you to be strong. We are going to cut these ties before they get back. I keep an extra key to the workshop under a brick in the corner to our left. We have to get over there somehow and try to cut these bands around our hands and feet. It's our only chance."

With that, we slowly began to scoot our chairs to the left, inches at a time......

CHAPTER 31

Allison Branch was always a bit crazy. She grew up in a home that was broken and her abusive father left her mother when she was eight. Hurt beyond belief, she could never trust men again. With her anxiety increasing as she was entering her teen years, she was increasingly living on a dangerous edge; she began to picture herself as the hero to avenge all the injustices of the world. She became intent upon making the lives of most of the men who attempted to come into her life, miserable. She couldn't keep boyfriends although many of them wanted to be with her.

She began to derive pleasure from cartoon like juvenile acts that raised the eyebrows of her teachers and her mother. Her mother kept defending her, trying to excuse her behavior. But as she was leaving high school, the only person she believed in or listened to was her tennis coach. She got a tennis scholarship and was trying to straighten out her life. It was her release, it was her one escape from feelings that she could not shake, the feelings of wanting to hurt others, the way she had been hurt by others. She had always wondered why she couldn't be like the rest of her friends, finding a guy, settling down and having kids. She wondered what made these other girls get picked? She was prettier, smarter and sexier than all of her friends, so why not me, she asked herself over and over.

When an injury ended her tennis career, she decided to work for a prosecutor in town. She was smart and efficient, but the work left her empty. She wanted to be able to avenge her ugly childhood so she decided to be a cop. Entering the police academy was tough on females. She immediately felt scorned by others, especially the male students. She really didn't care for the other female students. She despised them, except for one. The girl was young and spirited, just like her. It was why they bonded.

Their bond continued as they hung out together after hours and, occasionally, had drinks together. Their friendship became deeper and then became something more than just friendship. They had a special bond, as if they were meant to pursue the villains and evil-doers of this world. They were going to be a team, the two girls who explored each other in many ways, and in many ways becoming closer than sisters. But the young spirited girl was told to leave the academy over an incident with one of the instructors and, poof, Allison's friend was gone. God, she hated those arrogant assholes and Allison was going to get her revenge in many forms, maybe not at the academy, because she wasn't going to be driven out.

She would finish and she would finish at the top of her class. Someone was standing in the way of that happening, a good-looking guy, an arrogant jerk like the rest of them, Andy Marx still looked like he would finish ahead of her. He was smart, damn him. He had a way of looking inside people, breaking them down psychologically. It was Allison's only weakness, her fear of others who could break her down. Break her down and analyzing why she acted as she did. She kept him at arm's length, not wanting to have him get close and break *her* down. No male was ever going to do that. No one was breaking her down.

At academy graduation, Allison was down. She knew she was beaten by Marx. Marx had finished first and she was not happy about it. To show it and cause a scene would certainly doom her career before it even started. The day of graduation she politely shook hands and congratulated Marx. She had done it mostly against every hostile feeling that she held inside of her heart. But there would come a day, a day where he would be second to her, she thought. And that day Allison Branch would be number one and he would no longer cast any shadow over her.

Ironically, they had risen in the department and both made detective. They were partners together and Allison's insides were torn apart by this. They were equal partners, but she always thought she was better. This guy would slip and she would have her day in the sun. Patiently she waited...

Andy Marx dialed James Parson's number that had showed up on his cell. He felt that James was genuinely worried and it looked like he and Branch were getting ready to release to the press that Mike Parsons was missing.

James was at work, but saw that Marx's number was on the screen and stepped out of his office to take it.

"Thanks for calling back. I just had to talk to you about a feeling I have. I am feeling funny about Detective Branch. There just isn't any urgency in her voice about finding my brother. Especially for someone who was romantically interested in Mike," I explained.

"Not sure about that," Marx replied hesitantly. "I mean it's hard to go on a feeling, but what is it that you suspect?"

"I don't think she's being straight with me. I think she knows more than she is telling either you or me," James said thinking he might be stepping over the line.

"She's always been a pretty good cop. Do you think maybe you are jumping too quick on this? Maybe you need to just give us time to find out. It's very early in this investigation and we are looking into a few things. I'll be talking with her in a just a few minutes as I'm almost at the station. Look, I promise, I'll get back to you as soon as I hear something, okay?"

"Okay, but it sure seems odd that her main squeeze is missing and that she seemed so cool about it," James replied.

"Yeah, but you need to know that cops need to take the emotion out of things sometimes, especially when it involves someone close to you," Marx said, somewhat like James had offended him with his comment.

"Okay, I trust you, but please let me know if you find something out. We are close and I just have a real bad feeling about all of this."

"Will do," Marx responded as he hung up the phone. He pulled in the station and decided it was time for a little conversation with Branch. Marx was ready to do some psychological breaking down, as he too suspected something out of whack, as he always had with Branch. How James felt about Branch was sticking with Marx. The same kind of feeling Marx had the day they both graduated from the academy and she congratulated him for finishing first ahead of her. He had a hard time trusting her then and was really having a tough time doing that now. Something was definitely wrong and he was going to find out. After all, he did finish first.

CHAPTER 32

Katy and I had been fed with crackers and water, better than nothing and we were trying to figure out how to get out of this. We had tried once to struggle to our feet and possibly break our chairs providing us an edge with which to cut our banded wrists. Our attempts were unsuccessful. Our captors had just left and although, we had been fed, we were still weak and drugged, functioning poorly. I had to think harder, what am I missing? I know this place and I keep something in a corner that would help us, what is it, think, Mikey, think! Then it came to me.

"Katy, in the corner to my left, there is a corner shelf. I'm going to slide over and try to knock the shelf off with my head," I said, not confident at all that I could do it. "After I knock the shelf off maybe I can back up to one of the bolts and cut my bands on my wrists. Then I can cut you loose."

Mike, I don't know. I just hope you can," Katy

replied.

"We have to try now, tomorrow they may kill us. I'll make it. We won't survive if I don't."

I moved slowly across the concrete floor. The air was cold and stale as I fought to keep my senses sharp enough to do this. I had to make it. I'm a survivor. I inched closer until I awkwardly ran into the shelf. I ducked my head under the middle shelf and rose up quickly to dislodge the shelf from the stand. An edge slightly cut my left cheek and blood began to drip down the side of my face. *There, I got it! Now the hard part will be getting in a position to cut the band. Luckily the screw on the stand is the right height and I just need to work my hands up and down where the screw would cut it eventually. Just don't slice your own wrists, Mike.*

Carefully, I worked the band over the screw back and forth. Finally, it broke and my hands were free. I bent over and recovered the shelf and began working the edge of the shelf and cut the bands on my legs. I tried to stand but fell immediately. My legs were weak and my eyes blurry. I got to my knees and felt as though I was going to vomit.

"Katy, I'm bringing the shelf over there to cut you loose and we can get out of here." I said in a raspy tone, not recognizing my voice.

"Hurry, Mike, before they get back. I want out of here so bad."

"Just a few more minutes and we'll be gone," I replied as I crawled towards her.

I moved the metal edge of the shelf across her bands on her wrists and cut them, easier than my own and did the same for her legs. She hugged me and was crying.

"Katy, get a grip, we have got to make our way to the opening. We will open the door and get out. We don't have much time to waste. This is my lake place and I know where to go, we just need to get out. With no flashlight, we will have to stay close until we get to the house. We'll get my boat key and take the boat. It's cold but it will be faster. Just hope she starts, we will then get to a neighbor and call the police," I said really believing that we had **finally** after three days of fatigue, drug injections, and abuse we would get out. We were weak but we needed to keep going.

We made our way over and my ribs hurt fiercely with each step, breathing was difficult and my legs felt like lead weights.

"Okay, we're there. Now all we have to do is open the latch and get out. Then we get to the house, get the boat key and boat to the neighbors. I'll grab a couple of blankets for you and we take off from the dock," I was telling Katy. "Look, you have to be strong, my bartender friend, trust me, we are getting out of this."

"I'm ready, it's time to get out of here. You know they will be back," Katy said.

I reached for the latch, fumbling around until I grasped it, and turned it to the left releasing it in the open position. I pushed and ...*Shit, can't budge it. Something is wedged in the latch outside. We're trapped in and we were still prisoners.*

CHAPTER 33

*Hey Jude, don't make it bad, take a sad song and
make it better. The minute you let her into your
heart, then you can start, to make it better*
-The Beatles

I told Katy we were trapped and wedged in from
the outside, she fell into me weeping and begging
me to help her, to save her. I held her for what
seemed to be quite some time and then thought, *hey,
they can be back any minute. We have to do
something, plan B for night number three.*

"Mike, you have to come up with a plan, "she said
through tears. "You must know now how much I have
loved you. Why? Why her? You could have had me
any time. You'll never know how much I dreamed of
us, of you and me together. Then she stepped in, it
killed me on the inside."

"We can't talk about that now; we have to make a
plan. They'll be back and we'll have to do something,

something possibly violent to save ourselves. Our mind set has to be on that purpose. Look, I promise, we'll talk about it later, but right now, let's toughen up and get our heads on straight. They'll come back here and stick those needles in us again and make us non-functioning zombies again and then you know we'll be done. Worse they may just go ahead and kill us. I promise, we'll talk later."

And now for Plan B...

----▲----

Jerry was busy shuffling papers around and thinking that his business was going to survive. He had made plans with the Voice, plans that really couldn't fail if everyone did their jobs and didn't screw it up. He would make enough money to infuse into his business, he had ways to launder it and make it clean. There was never any need to tell his wife about this. She had always felt his business was legitimate and that he made it through hard work. But this time, he had to go under the table and make it work. He had big plans and the Voice was helping him achieve his agenda, little by little, and soon, his plan would come to fruition.

He picked up the phone and called the Voice. The Voice answered quickly, "Yeah?"

"Jerry, here. I think you left out a few details in this note that I am curious about. I get to wondering if you're really going to come through for me," Jerry said with a hint of suspicion in his own voice.

"Look, I put you in an awesome position to get everything you want. You know I am the one making your fondest wishes come true," the Voice said in a half sarcastic tone."

"Don't mess it up. I got friends and they're not real

nice."

"Don't threaten me with that big man stuff. I got this covered, but you don't need to intimidate me. I don't scare easily. I've dealt with plenty of people like you. This stuff is going to be easy, trust me."

"It had better be. Everyone has a lot to lose here. Just make sure the plan works. I'll be in touch."

Jerry hung up and rose from his desk and began pacing about the office. *This has to work, but I have to say, I have never been more prepared to take the biggest risk in my life. I have to play this one out. I'm going to make my life right again, going to sink that last putt.*

And with that, Jerry got his heavy outdoor clothes, his pistol, and made sure all was ready on his end. Part Two was going to happen.

CHAPTER 34

I was sure they would come back soon so we had to think fast. That male voice, I knew it but I was struggling to place it. We were up against three figures. The figures had drugged us, kicked me, punched Katy, and would probably come back for that last dose of drugs to end our lives. They would have lights and we wouldn't, so we needed some kind of surprise tactic.

"When they come through the door, one of us probably me, needs to be behind the steps. You will have to sit in the chair and pretend you are still tied up in the chair," I said through searing rib cage pain. "I am hoping all three don't show up this time, we can take two but three will be much harder."

"Mike, what will I defend myself with?" Katy asked, not knowing if there was anything she would be able to do to stop one of them.

"Take the shelf apart and we will have metal clubs, go for the nose and head area as many times as you can. I'll take one out from the back and finish the other for you. If there is a third, we just have to fight with that much more rage."

Katy nodded. She looked unsure as far as I could tell in the semi-darkness.

I moved closer to her and grabbed her hand. "Look, you know I have your back. We just have to really rely on each other. Our lives depend on it."

Her hand was cold and clammy with nervous sweat. I squeezed it gently. "Katy, we will get out of this. We will talk later, I promise."

She laid her head on my shoulder and put her arms around my neck. Despite all we had been through, her touch was heavenly even though we were probably both scared, we held onto each other for what seemed to be minutes, we had no idea if what we planned would work or if we would even make it out alive. To hold her for just a while made us both a little more secure. It may end up being the final minutes of our lives.

We began to tear up the shelf, bending and breaking pieces apart. Some of the ends of the side rails were broken, leaving jagged edges at the end. I gave two pieces to Katy just in case one was taken from her or she lost her grip. I kept two for me and placed another behind the steps.

We took our places and we waited for their return. It would be too late if we went to our positions as soon as we heard them, so in place we waited. We talked across the room, but I told Katy to be silent when you she heard the first noise.

"Why didn't you ever make a play for me, Mike?" she asked. "You do know that I love you? I always have, I was just weak and didn't want to be turned down. I was afraid you wouldn't want me."

"When we went to the Lake House together, I was

thinking that maybe it was possible, but I didn't want to make that assumption. You have to know how awkward I really am around women, you were so much easier to be around, but I thought we were good friends."

"You love that detective, don't you?"

'I don't know. There are times when I think I do but I am not sure."

Not sure, Katy. He said not sure. Maybe, just maybe I still have a chance.

"You know, I think I could make you happy. I think you would like to have someone love you, like you always say you need to be loved." Katy began to cry and I heard her sniffles. "I listened to you, all your stories and each time I put myself in the place of the one you should choose. I truly felt so good each time I saw you walk into the bar. I just have to tell you this. I know it doesn't matter now. But please know, if we get out of here, just give me one chance, just one."

I was quiet and did not respond. I didn't want to give her any false hope. I was still feeling Allison and that was my first instinct as of now. I am just wishing she and Marx could get here and get us out of here.

"Look," I said. "This situation requires us to focus on getting out of here. I'm going to do all I can to make sure that is what happens. I do promise you, we will talk, but my first thought is to protect you and get you out of this mess I got you into."

The handle rattled and we both froze. I had never even thought about an Armageddon day in my life. I never thought I would be here, but for Plan B, its time is now.

CHAPTER 35

Jerry drove down the newly plowed road waiting for the Voice to call. He had waited for this moment for quite some time now. He was anxious and was ready to rid himself of the demons that possessed him since Sheila's death. The business would survive, Margaret and he would be normal again, and he would have what he wanted most.

His phone ring startled him from his thoughts and for a minute he froze. He picked up on the second ring.

"All set?" the Voice asked.

"I'm prepared. I've waited for this for a while," Jerry replied.

"We meet where I told you. Don't be late as everything is timed. People are in place and everything gets done today." The Voice knew what to do and had everything planned down to the second and a backup in case someone screwed up. The Voice was smart, arrogant and sure it was all going to work.

"Okay, I will meet you in twenty minutes."

Jerry hung up and a strange sense of excitement was beginning to build inside him. No business deal, no other event in his life had stirred his consciousness to this level. He took a few deep breaths and tried to relax. This is it. The one moment he chose just a while back. The moment that would relieve his stress, his anxiety, his sleepless nights and allow him to be who he used to be.

Andy Marx got another call from James Parsons. James was pleading with him to at least go with him. Marx replied that it was unsafe to take civilians with you on duty. Right now, he was on duty.

"I'm just getting ready to call my partner and we will go take a look around together," Marx told James. "No sense in your physical involvement here. It would all be against policy."

James began to think something strange about Marx now. He was after all paranoid about everything at this point. "Look, just please call if you have something new, but I would check his lake place out. I'll text you the address. I almost went there myself," James said with hopeful urgency.

"Okay, look, Branch and I will go check it out. Just stay clear until we can get something."

"Alright, alright, I'll be waiting."

Marx hung up and dialed Branch. He let the phone ring and it went to voicemail.

"Marx here. Hey, give me a call as soon as possible. I think we need to get out to his lake place and check it over better. Something about this just has me thinking. We'll talk soon."

Marx hung up and then headed for the station, hoping that Branch was busy in the office. When he got there, Branch was not in. He asked around but no one had seen her or heard from her all day after she checked out of the station. Marx had a funny feeling and the feeling was making his gut hurt. He was going out to the lake place with her or without her. He went back to his car and began to thirty-mile trek out of town.

He picked up the phone and once more dialed Branch. She picked up on the second ring.

"Hey, I have a hunch about that lake place of Mike Parsons. Where can we meet? I'm headed that way now," Marx said.

"I can make it there in twenty minutes," Branch replied. "I'll just meet you there."

"Okay, I got the address from his brother, James. Take 65 to it, it's faster."

"Okay," Branch said. "I'll see you in a few."

Marx felt a bit better as he hung up. He had a gut feeling that still irked him. But, he had to trust his partner. They had done a lot together and apprehended a few bad dudes as partners. Surely, she was okay he thought. Probably nothing, but still he was going to be careful.

Branch hung up and what she didn't tell Marx was that she was already there at the lake place. She had been there for an hour. She had her own plans and she wasn't letting Marx beat her to it. Not any more, not this time or next time, not ever again! She was going to be number one and the Voice had made the master plan, she had stalked, she had evaded everyone's suspicions and was smarter than all these people. She, Allison Branch, the Voice, would have all the things denied her. She would do away with that bastard Marx and the bartender, and most of all that Mike Parsons, yes, that same Mike Parsons that didn't choose her many years ago...

CHAPTER 36

I heard the piece wedging the door click metal on metal. It was slowly being removed and the soon the latch would open. Hiding beneath the stairs, I could hear one of the voices. "They should still be drugged up, but they are going to need another shot. Then we will take them out of here and let him have them, and we are going to have our revenge. Finally, we get rid of these people and then we will have our justice."

"Wait," a farther and fainter voice said. "Not everyone is in place, yet. Give me five more minutes and then go in. Remember be careful going in. I know they are tied up, but you never know, we can't blow this. We are all going to be rich, but you have to do this thing right. Give them the shots, drag them up out of the shelter, use the duct tape and tie them up. You know what to do with the girl and then you know what to do with him."

"Yes, we've got you. It should be easy enough. But

what about your partner?"

"Don't worry, I have that figured out. I'll take care of Marx. Just give me five minutes."

Okay, take that, buddy boy. I know that voice. Oh, my god, it's Branch! She's the one who set me up. But why, what did I do to her? Someone in my life earlier? Couldn't be, I would have remembered her. Think, think! I felt anger, shock, and stupid. Once again, one more wrong choice in life and it was about to end me. I have to save Katy and get her out of here. That's the least I could do. Don't change plans, but it is good to know that there are only two. It wouldn't be Branch. I would deal with her later I'm sure, but first things first.

Five minutes seemed like an eternity. I was hoping Katy could come through. I didn't want to doubt her, but I just didn't know...

Marx was driving now at a good clip, skidding on the gravel road. He couldn't let her be ambushed. Still he slowed his vehicle and stopped, getting out to walk the last hundred yards. He could see the house in the distance, spotted her car, but she was nowhere in sight. He walked slowly through the gate and drew his gun, careful not to make too much noise. He edged closer to the house, moving from tree to tree, careful as his training had told him he should be. He stopped and peered at the windows, hoping to catch some movement or shadows letting him know where she was. Seeing nothing, he moved from the last tree to the front entrance.

"Drop it and don't' turn around." Marx dropped his service pistol and immediately knew his hunch was right, even though he wished it wasn't true.

"I was really hoping my hunch was wrong, but it wasn't. This is the one time I didn't play smart enough. Looks like you finally got back at me," Marx said in his best psychologist voice.

"Just shut up! I've put up with you long enough. I was better than you, I always was. You just had sucked up to all the trainers, and that's why you beat me, not because you were better," she said through clenched teeth. "Keep walking to the back slowly. Move quickly and you're dead." She picked up his gun keeping a safe distance from him.

Marx had to think and think fast or he was dead. He had worked a couple of cases where people had killed out of jealousy. It made people do strange things way out of ordinary behavior. He walked slowly and she matched each step until he was on the back porch. Holding the gun on him she waved him inside. They slowly walked in together.

"In the laundry room, just ahead," she said still following carefully.

"Look, Branch, you won't get away with this. Even if you kill me, they'll know it's you. Everyone will know," Marx said trying to remain calm.

"They won't know. They'll never pin that on me. I'm a cop and no one is suspecting me. You're the one I have always hated. You and Parsons. It's going to be my pleasure to do away with you both. "Then my life will be better. I already set up Parson's father in law. He will be the one they pin the crime on and they won't find you, they won't find any of you. I'll be the hero, solved the crime, get the promotion you thought you would get. Hell, I beat you Marx, just when it counted."

"C'mon, Allison, you won't hold up, you never do. Just like the time you let me down and didn't fire at that pimp who was holding the club over me and about to beat me to death. And when you did, you missed on purpose. You wanted him to kill me."

Allison had had enough of this guy. Too many years, too much frustration. She easily squeezed off two rounds hitting Marx in the shoulder and the hip. He went down fast bleeding profusely from both wounds. Allison thought he would bleed out, but she quickly duct-taped his hands, feet and gagged him. She would come back and deal with the body. She had to take care of the other one first. She closed the door and was headed back out towards the shed...

CHAPTER 37

They entered slowly, the first one, little Breanne, hopped down off the ladder without seeing me. *Now!* I jabbed the metal piece into the back of her thigh. Katy swung hard and connected with Breanne's head and she went down fast. The second attacker ran for the woods, not allowing me to see who it might have been.

"Up the ladder, Katy, quick!" I yelled and pushed her as she scrambled up. Breanne was on all fours bleeding profusely from her head. In the light I saw her face and it froze me. Of course, Brenda's little sister from high school. I recognized her as her features had not changed that much. I swung again and hit her neck, cutting her again. She fell flat again and up the steps I went. I grabbed Katy's hand and yelled, "Run!" We took off, running fast as I pulled her along.

"Over there, my boat house is down that path. Stay in the trees," I said panting heavily.

"Mike, I have to stop. I can't go further." Katy was sweating and it was cold out.

"We have to move. They'll be after us and we just have to get to my boat house, get my keys and head out on the boat to get to safety," I said breathing heavily myself.

Crack! A shot zinged the tree we were hiding behind. I saw two people running at us. I know we didn't kill her, but surely, with the metal in her leg, wasn't chasing us, too.

"Katy, be quick, we need to go over there," pointing to my right. "There's a small ravine just over that crest. Roll into it and run up the ravine. It's a way to distract them. We'll go back around my house and down to the boat house. It's our only chance."

We ran towards the ravine and dove for it. We crawled up the ravine as a few bullets grazed the top of the crest. We couldn't crawl too far as they would be closing in on us.

"Run, Katy, you have to keep going."

We ran as fast as we could until we ran back around the back side of my house. We had bought time and we might be able to make it back around and back to the boat house now. I had a gun inside but I didn't think I had time to get it.

"Katy, wait here. I'll be quick. I am going inside and get my gun. Then we'll make a run for it. Don't move, if she comes before I get out, come inside and we'll deal with it from the inside."

I entered the house and headed for my room and to get my hand gun from the side closet. In a hurry, I didn't notice anything strange or out of place. I got it and turned to leave my room and headed towards the back porch and I froze when I saw Branch holding her arm around Katy's throat with her pistol to her head, little Breanne, battered and bleeding by her side.

"Drop the gun and kick it to me, Mike," Branch said. I dropped it and slid it over to Breanne who was obviously angry and would have shot us both if Branch gave the go ahead.

"I'd let you kill them both, but we have other plans for them. You've done well, my dear. We'll get rid of these two and then we'll collect our cash. Easy money and we can live the life we always wanted to. See, Mike, you could have had me back then, back then when you didn't know me. Back when you picked that bar fly instead of me. You really don't recognize me, do you? I didn't have blonde hair then, it was jet black. I was sitting at the next table from you and that bitch. You, some hot shot lawyer out cheating all over town on your wife. You could have had me, but no you chose that bimbo. Why? Because she was blonde? You know me, you just don't remember, because you didn't know my name. You had seen me before, you know that sexy brunette that worked in Curry's office? Yeah, you remember now. You hit on me, you bought me a drink, and then that bitch called you over to her. Too fuzzy for you? Oh no, you remember now. It's too late now. See, the orange lipstick said it all. You were never going to find out who did it. Now you know and the funny thing is, it won't matter, you will be dead soon."

"Look, I'm sorry I didn't know. How could I know? I said nervously eyeing her with Katy in her grip.

"Just something to throw you off, Mikey," Branch replied. "Cold as hell, I know, but revenge is best served cold, lover. You couldn't have it easy, and for me this was so fulfilling. Bad karma, right? See I DO believe in destiny. My destiny was to screw you over really bad. I got my wish. Now move it. Out the door, both of you. Either one of you makes a noise and you're dead. We're going down to the boathouse,

Mikey. I have a friend I want you to meet."

We walked out the door, slowly trudging to what I knew was our certain death now. We were out of ideas and no weapons. Breanne was trailing closely behind, holding my weapon on us and Allison behind me.

We made it to the dock and boathouse. Breanne reached into a bag on the dock and produced a roll of duct tape. *Oh great, tied up again!*

Branch held the gun on us as Breanne wrapped up my wrists behind my back. She did the same for Katy and we were once again the captives, ready for execution...

CHAPTER 38

James was driving fast, nearing the gate of the lake property. He saw cars first and began to slow down. He put the car in park, shut it off and got into the trunk and pulled out his deer rifle, the only weapon he ever handled confidently as a civilian. He ran to the house getting behind trees when he could. He got to the front door and tried the handle. It was locked! Quickly, he ran to the back and saw footprints wet and muddy from snow. There were several, something bad had obviously happened and he slowly began to check the rooms one by one.

Going down the hall he suddenly stopped and saw blood running under the laundry room door onto the hallway floor. *Oh my God, what am I going to see in here he thought.* He slowly opened the door holding his rifle and then positioned it to shoot. He kicked the door the rest of the way open and pointed the firearm. There he found Marx, bleeding badly. He undid the gag and immediately Marx whispered, "Call 911, I'm hurt bad. Get them here fast, then try and stop the bleeding. They have your brother, and another person. They're going to the dock, they plan on killing him. Get me settled and tourniquet my leg. Then chase them down. Leave me your phone and cut my hands and feet free, I'll get on the line with the 911 operator."

James ran to the kitchen and got a steak knife to cut the tape on Marx. Then he found two towels, pressing them hard into his shoulder wound. He found the broom and broke it in two and made a tourniquet with it. He cinched it tight above the thigh wound. He then dialed 911 and handed the phone to Marx.

"Hurry, go before it's too late. I will get the cops here. Go!"

James took off and headed down the path, moving carefully as not to be seen ...

Now that they had us tied up, Branch made us walk to my boat.

"I would like you to meet a friend of mine and your captain for the rest of this day," Allison said as cold breath from us all hit the frigid air. "He's been waiting for you."

We turned the corner...*Oh shit, this just can't be!*

"Hello, Mike. You look so surprised," Jerry laughed. "I wish I could take a picture of your face. Heard the gunfire and the chase, but I guess all is in good order now and we are going for a cruise."

Yes, the male voice. That was it. He was the other male. Holy shit, we are in trouble here.

"Jerry, you know, I didn't hurt Sheila. She hurt herself, she had problems."

"You were her problem, asshole. Now you have

become my problem. Easy problem though, as we just go for a little ride and I rid myself of this problem. Detective lady, she got her revenge, now it's my turn. Step aboard, and let's cruise." He threw his head back and laughed like a mad man.

Okay, I'm going to die, knowing the story, just not why this all took place. Katy was frightened, her eyes, oh my, now I couldn't even take care of her like before. Tears ran from her eyes and it was my fault, once again, Mr. Awkward was not coming to the rescue. Not this time...

"Okay, the cash, Jerry," Branch said quickly. Jerry handed over the small bag to Allison. "Alright, nice doing business with you. Let's go, Breanne. Damn Marx got in the way. He's collateral damage. Let's go finish the guy off. Then we get out of here. My police work is done. I could have worked out the promotion, but too much happened. We're just going to make a dash for it, take the cash and get out of the country."

"Have a nice time with your bimbo bartender and your father-in-law," Branch said as she and Breanne began to make their way back up towards the house from the boathouse and dock.

Jerry started the motor and the boat began to pull away from the dock. Katy and I are sitting ducks to another mad individual. This one would most assuredly end us.

James was already running from the house and Branch saw him quickly. She told Breanne to get in the woods and let him by. They hid behind a large brush pile until he had passed.

James ran onto the dock only to see Mike's boat pulling out from the cove. He thought he knew where to go next and sprinted down the wooded bank as fast as he could. He had to be careful not to stumble with his rifle. He ran hard for the bluff as it was coming into his sight line. He had to get in front of that boat.

Jerry held the gun on Katy and me. We were freezing in the cold air and were shivering.

"Is this your new playmate, Mike? Ran around on my little girl, didn't you? Still doing it, too. Wow, you just have no respect for anyone or anything do you? You know how much I have waited for this moment? The moment that avenges my daughter's death?"

"Jerry, you know how confused she was," I replied. "There were times when I wasn't sure if she loved me anymore, you had to have seen it."

"She always loved you, and really I thought you were the best thing that ever happened to her. But you let her down. Just like you let everyone else down in your life. Just like you are going to let this girl down. You're really not the golden boy you think you are. Everyone you bring in to your pitiful life gets destroyed, somehow."

"Jerry, you can't bring her back, this won't make that happen," I said trying to buy any small amount of time that I could.

"I think we are in the middle of the lake now. Just as good a time as any. Not listening any longer. You are a dead man..."

▲

James had made it to the bluff. It was high and overlooked the lake, presenting a beautiful view for lake inhabitants. Being ex-military would serve James well in this scenario. He got into a laying shooting position. His gun was loaded and ready, and James relaxed his body. He had to relax at the moment he would squeeze the trigger. The boat was coming in to view and James started to sight in the scenario. Jerry had his pistol at his side and he could see his face, angry, distorted with each word. There would be not much time to lose, as the moment was getting intense. He had made this shot before in the war in Iraq. He had made this shot easily in the woods hunting deer. He just could not miss *this one.*

Jerry lifted his gun and, closing my eyes, seemed like the right thing to do.

I spouted the Lord's Prayer in my mind and was getting ready to meet my maker...

CHAPTER 39

Slowly James breathed in and out until he felt totally relaxed and still. Jerry raised his pistol and aimed at Mike. NOW! James lightly squeezed off the shot during exhale. The crack was loud and he watched the shooter's gun fall as Jerry raised his hands. The bullet did its work quickly and efficiently, killing its target almost instantly. Jerry fell over the side and into the water, floating, with blood spilling out quickly around him.

I could feel nothing as the loud crack sounded as my eyes were closed. I expect to feel pain but there is nothing. I open my eyes and see the body floating. Blood is all around it, blood spatter in the boat. Katy grabs me and is in-between screams and sobs, almost to the point of delirium. I hold her close to me, in shock, cold and shivering. I try to make sense of it all and try to calm her delirium. Sirens are blaring as the water patrol boat is approaching. Someone saved us and I had a hunch of who that might be.

_____▲_____

James ran back towards the lake house. He was hoping to find the police there. He was hoping to find Marx okay and living. Sirens blaring, he froze and hid behind a brush pile. He saw the two females running towards the house. The sirens were still blaring and the vehicles erupted through the closed gate and came to a skidding stop. The officers quickly sprang out of their vehicles and got into defense position behind their open doors. The women dove to the side of the house avoiding the first bullet spray. They would soon surround Branch and Jackson. Their only chance was to get inside and claim Marx as a hostage, if he was still alive. Allison broke the window and the two crawled inside cutting themselves on the glass on the way in. All of this in James' view was like a movie, like it couldn't possibly happen.

The final contest between Branch and Marx would now take place. Once again, Allison had sold Marx short. She was sure he would be dead or near it now. Police had surrounded the house and were ready to go in. The quiet was chilling, and Allison and Breanne ran to the laundry room to find Marx. What she and Breanne found was the pistol that was in Marx's leg holster pointed at them and they had no time to react.

"Looks like I win again," and Marx fired four quick shots and each of them found the mark. They each took one shot to the head and the chest, dropping them immediately. His toughness, his planning and his superior ambition had kept him alive and he had once again proven to be the better officer than

Branch. He was exhausted and in bad shape, but he had prevailed. The officers storming the house kicked the guns away from the two bodies.

"Get the medics in here quick," the lead officer called out. He held the other two at gunpoint and they would try to save all three, Branch, Marx, and Breanne. The medics were working fast especially with Marx. He had lost a lot of blood and his condition was critical. He had passed out. All three bodies were being loaded into the ambulance as James dropped his weapon and raised his hands. Two officers, approaching cautiously, had him kneel on the ground as he was cuffed and taken to the patrol car.

The nightmare was over as Katy and I were taken aboard the water patrol craft. Another officer took control of my vessel. We had several things to sort out and my boat was being considered a crime scene and would be under investigation. *It had to be James. I just knew it, but how? What did he know? He was the only person I know who could shoot like that. It had to be him.*

We were taken from the dock and into custody of two more officers on the path to the house. There was so much to sort out. But first where is James? He had to be here and I was hoping he was not hurt. As we walked up, we did not see him.

We were put in to one of the three squad cars that I could see. The warmth was welcoming. I could see two ambulances screeching out of the gate and heading to the hospital. Geez, it can't be James. Then I spotted him, head down in the other squad car. Hell, they arrested him, but my thought was it had to be James that made that shot that killed Jerry. He would have to answer questions, but Katy and I knew that he was defending us and we were witnesses. We would know how to help James out of this mess. We were all going for a ride. We would be going to the station and the police would question us to make their reports. Then the reports will go to prosecutors and they will consider this evidence and decide if a complaint or case would be made. Who is it? Who is dead and who is alive? Branch, Marx, Breanne?

For James, there would be the law. Was he acting in the interest of preserving life and property of an individual? I could help him with that, but he would also need a defense attorney. The whole thing was confusing and there was much more to do. The road ahead was long.

The ride to the station was long and very quiet. Katy could not stop her tears as she was still in shock and would be taken to the hospital for treatment. I supposed I would be treated as well. The case to me was so jumbled, so confusing. I was hoping to somehow get this dark cloud removed from above my head. I was sick, tired and confused. At this very moment, I would be willing to just check out of this life.

CHAPTER 40

The local headlines and TV news stories were buzzing with headlines and breaking news reports. Local cop arrested, three injured critically, and kidnapped victims hospitalized. I am in ICU and being treated for shock, drugs and other injuries. Katy is also in the room next to mine doing the same. I could not speak to her and wondered when we would be out of here. I hurt all over, and I know she must be struggling as well. I could only wonder about the others.

It was ironic that I was back in St. Luke's, the place where my ex-wife had passed away. I felt haunted and trapped. I wanted out. I knew I would be stuck here until I could heal. I had no one. James was under arrest, Katy was in another room, and all I would have for the next few days would be doctors, nurses, and cops talking to me.

I thought of the wild turn of events and what had put me here. I felt strange physically. I was nervous and edgy as well as in great pain. I wish I was back in the hole and they would give me another shot. I began to sweat and somehow, I knew I needed to shake this new-found addiction. I would, once again, have to fight something. Would I have to overcome a mild addiction to drugs? All I know is that I wish I could have a shot. Any shot. Any drug...

Katy was in better physical shape than most of us. She thought of Mike and was wondering if he was thinking of her. She had been terrified by these events. A doctor and a psychologist had already been in to see her.

Katy was dreaming in her sleep. She had seen the gun pointed at Mike and had heard the awful crack. In her dream she had seen the bullet from Jerry's gun hit first Mike and another shot that hit her. They were falling and spinning and unable to breathe. She opened her mouth to scream, but there was no air only water. She was drowning and just wanted someone to save her. She could see Mike's hand reaching for her, but he was too far. He could not reach her...

Katy woke up and was surprised at her surroundings. She was out of breath and sweating profusely. She screamed for help and a nurse arrived quickly as a police guard allowed the nurse in.

"There now, easy, young lady. You just had a bad dream," the nurse said as she gently put her hand on Katy's arm. "You need to breathe, slow down and catch your breath."

"I keep having dreams, terrible dreams," Katy said.

"You just need to relax. I'll see if I can get you a sedative so you can rest."

"Thank you," Katy replied.

Where is Mike? I need Mike. I have to see him. It

would help me. I need him...

I needed to talk to Katy. We needed to get some things right in our heads before we were questioned. Talking about this would help but it could also trigger bad responses from Katy. How long would it be? I had to find things out about James. I needed to see him and try to find out what trouble he might be in. I didn't have to wait long as the Chief of the Milwaukee Police Department walked into my room.

"Mr. Parsons, my name is Neal Underwood. I am Chief of Police, Milwaukee PD, and was wondering if you were up to a few questions? I know you have been through a rough ordeal and I will try to fill you in on where things stand at the moment," he said.

"Sure, I'm okay," I replied. "I really want to know what's happening. This has all been a crazy time and my mind may not recall everything, but I sure do have some things and some people I need to know about."

"Good. First let me fill you in on people. Your ex-father-in-law is deceased. Second, your friend, Katy, is resting in another room on this floor. Your brother, James, is currently being held in connection with your father-in-law's death. You, as a prosecutor, do understand the law when it comes to private citizens taking situations into their own hands. So, you know he has some problems there. Third, Detective Marx has some serious wounds, but he is stable and in intensive care. Detective Branch and a friend, Breanne Jackson, are both in critical condition. They may not make it," he said looking down at his shoes.

"You can understand how devastating this all is, but I will try to recall as much as I can," I replied. Underwood took out a pad and pencil and asked his first question.

"What can you tell me about your time with

Branch? I am aware of the situation with your ex-wife, but we thought she had studied the case and worked very hard to try and solve it. It appears that she has had some trouble and from what we can get from Marx, who actually shot her, she was jealous of his position in the department. It was a situation that went all the way back to the academy. She also could have been involved in a drug ring in an effort to get enough cash to skip the country. But first, she had a plan to hurt you. Any reasons she may have had to do that?"

"Well, it's a long story but as she investigated my ex-wife's death further, I was under the impression she was trying to help Sheila's parents and me solve the case and get to the bottom of Sheila's stalker. I did have a short relationship with her, but certainly I was fooled by her intent. I actually thought I was falling in love with her. I was at her house when she was called out, and I went for a walk and was struck in the head and knocked cold. I wake up and I'm in a cold damp cellar, which as you know turned out to be my storm shelter at the lake place. Katy goes out there to look for me and they grab her, too. They had us both tied up in the shelter. There were three of them holding us. One was a man, who turned out to be Jerry Linhart. Katy and I have a confrontation with Breanne Jackson and another attacker. We disabled them and were going to my house to get my gun, and then Branch and Jackson come in and grab Katy. They make me give up the gun and she tells me how I rejected her once when she was working for attorneys in town. I didn't remember her as she did not have blonde hair then. She said I chose another woman in a bar and left her. I could not remember. Then she delivers us to Linhart on my boat. Jerry hands over cash to Allison and Breanne and takes off with Katy and me aboard.

When we reach the middle of the lake, he raised his gun to shoot me, but then a loud rifle shot rings out and I thought he had shot me but I felt nothing. I open my eyes and he's in the water, blood all over the place. Then the water patrol picks us up."

"Were you aware that the little one, Breanne Jackson, was with Branch at the academy?"

"No, I had no idea."

"Well, she was let go, but she and Branch had remained friends. Appears that they may have been in on this together. I can't say much more, but this investigation will be intensive for several reasons. Problems remain and your testimony will be important. Seems like your ex father-in-law was involved in the drug market. So, there are probably accomplices out there and since we also think Branch and Jackson were involved with the drug thing, you and Katy will be under protective custody."

"Well, it makes sense. They stuck us with needles and kept us drugged while we were there. We just had enough wits about us to ambush them when they came for us. Not sure what that means going forward." *I wanted to say, I think I'm hooked on the stuff and could use a shot right now, but I kept it to myself.*

"Look I'm curious, about the notes left in your condo. Who do you think left them?"

"It could have been Breanne, maybe Branch," I said pensively. "Just not sure I know."

"Do you think Branch and Jackson were planning on killing you?"

"Yes, in our conversation she said as much. She said I didn't pick her. She said it was her destiny to 'screw me over' really bad. Look, I'm not feeling the best. Can we continue this another time? "

"Sure," Underwood replied. "But a lot of info is

sensitive and we don't want to drag this out. We want to get this to the prosecutor as soon as we can."

"I understand, but can you do me one favor?"

"Sure."

"Could you check with personnel and see if I can talk to Katy O'Neal. She's a friend and I feel like I need to help support her."

"I'll see what I can do." With that, Underwood left the room.

I really needed to talk to Katy...and I really need a shot...

CHAPTER 41

I picked up the hospital phone and called Monica. She is in a panic and told the story of James' arrest. The panic in her voice made me hurt, and I wondered how once again, everyone I touched was now in some sort of trouble.

"Monica, listen, I can get my hands on $50,000 for bail. Listen to me, it will be alright. Police have been here questioning me. We just need to be honest and get through this. Get a hold of Larry Fredericks and get him on retainer for James. He's the best you'll find around here. We will get James out and start his defense. Don't worry, we'll make it right for him. Call me later when Fredericks gives you an answer."

Monica was crying and said," I 'm scared, really scared. We can't lose him."

"I know, I'm scared too, but we'll make it. I know what we have to do. I just need to get out of here." I told her to take care of herself and call me back.

Just then, a uniformed nurse wheeled Katy into my

room. Her eyes were somewhat sunken and tired, as if she didn't sleep well. The nurse wheeled her by my bed and left. I could see the uniform cop outside my door. Our conversation would not be private.

Katy was looking weak and vulnerable, but a slight smile was creeping across her lips. I could tell this episode had taken its toll on her. Katy had always considered herself weak and she was going to need all the help she could get. Feeling bad for her, I took her hand and she smiled a thin smile that told me how tired she was.

"Katy, I just can't tell you how sorry I am that you got involved in this. I had no idea that all this would happen. Now is not the time for the talk you wanted to have, but it is the time for me to check on you and let you tell me how you are and what you are experiencing from this horrible trail of events."

I looked at her, almost begging her to say something, anything, but tears began to stream down her soft cheeks.

"I don't where to start. I'm so tired and so exhausted, but I had to see you. I know I shouldn't have tried to put myself into this investigation, but I had to. To me, you are so important, I had to know what had happened to you," she said looking down at her hands. "You know I wanted to tell you how I felt so many times, but I couldn't. I thought you would reject me."

I reached up, wiping the tears from her face. "It's okay, it's going to be okay. I am going to see you get everything you need to recover from this. I will help you if you let me. We'll still have to go through the court cases, that alone will take some time. I will be there for you every step. When they question you, it will be on your own. I won't be able to sit through that with you. But for everything else I will be there," I said, wondering just how much I was committing to.

"I was so scared, not knowing what would happen. The kidnapping, escaping, being caught again. I almost thought that my life was over. Mike, I just need someone to tell me what to do, someone to help me. There is just so much inside me right now, but I'm so tired."

"Look, I'll call the nurse and get her to take you back. I know how much stress you must feel. We both feel that. We both need time, but like I promised, we will talk about things when this is done."

I just don't know if I am giving her too much hope. I really like her, but just not in that way. I will do what I said, I would be there for her, but our lives would have to be rebuilt from this nightmare at some point. Right now, that rebuild for me would not include Katy being more than my good friend...

The nurse came in and asked Katy if she was ready to return. Katy nodded yes and she began to wheel her around. Katy gave me one last glance that would remain burned into my soul for quite some time. A look that pleaded for me to want her, that she needed me and that wheeling out of my room was hurting her. This ordeal would be the final straw that would decide what I was all about. The question kept burning in my mind, *"Will I ever find my redemption?"*

CHAPTER 42

Fighting for their lives were Breanne Jackson and Allison Branch. The surgery for Branch was intensive and lasted several hours. There was a lot of internal damage that made her condition very critical. Luckily her head shot had only been a glancing blow that left her with no serious head wound. They wheel her into intensive care as she is hooked up to a respirator, with several tubes connected to her. There is no one there in the waiting room waiting for her, checking on her condition. She is going to fight this life and death battle on her own.

Breanne, on the other hand, was losing that battle, her blood pressure had become dangerously low, and breathing was shallow. Within minutes, a priest was summoned to give her the last rites. Outside in the waiting room was her sister Brenda. Brenda had come for her. It was her little sister, and she had always been there for her. She was there now. No one questioned her, and no one really thought she was involved. Underwood was watching and keeping an eye on this one. He knew it was Breanne's sister and she would certainly be a person of interest. But for now, he just had a plain clothes officer watch her from a distance. Underwood would talk to her later.

Breanne's fight was nearly over, her sister was called in to be with her. Breanne and she had only each other. Brenda was shaken and upset and suddenly Breanne quit breathing. They began CPR but to no avail and Breanne passed away. Brenda sank along the wall of the room until she was on her knees sobbing incessantly. The priest and a doctor held her up and took her away from this scene. Brenda Jackson had lost her sister. She had escaped the ordeal at the lake and had made it home before she had gotten the call. She had rushed to the hospital for Breanne, but it was over, and she would need to stay silent. In her mind, she had already thought of killing Mike Parsons. It was his fault. He had caused this.

―――▲―――

The third fight for life was taking place for Andy Marx. Marx was physically in great shape before the shootings but had lost a lot of blood. His doctors had done extremely well and he was also lucky that the wounds were not critical. He was in serious condition, but he would live. Waiting for him were his parents and his younger sister. He had support, and he would need them for his recovery.

One dead, one fighting for life and one was going to make it for sure. My brother was being held in Milwaukee and his wife, Monica, almost delirious. Katy and I would heal but the mental issues we were going to have would be severe.

Amidst all of this, I am once again feeling the grip

of the hand called depression. What has my life been? Where is it, exactly, that I stand? Each soul wanders through this life seeking only the best of themselves, but almost always they fall victim to adversity, embarrassment, or bad karma. Some of the souls survive it all. Some of the souls never are quite the same again. The events of our lives mold us. It is adversity that makes us get better or worse. We are all judged on how we handle those things. For me, I just don't know where I am at right now.

Staring out the window into the cold Wisconsin night, I see the shimmering lights that seem to be only dimly lighting what they are intended to illuminate. The light needs to change and become bright again. But how, and much more importantly, why am I even thinking that is what I need? My next two months will indeed make me or break me. I needed a bright light, someone or something to show me that what I wanted to be all along is what I could be. But all I see right now is a dimly lit street lamp outside my hospital room window and a dimly lit life needing a re-start.

Sleep did not come easy. I was restless and had flashbacks about the past week. I couldn't get the look on Katy's face out of my head. I was worried about James and Monica. I was worried for Marx's health. So much I did not know and so much that I could not change. I thought of Allison Branch and how someone whom I have affected in some way, again, is suffering or has suffered for some time. Her life hangs in the balance.

I fell for her. Was I that stupid? What is it about me that seems to create unhappiness and confusion in others? It seems the only ones that I can trust are James, Monica, and Katy. Finally sleep came to me and when I awoke I was about to get all the news from Captain Underwood...

CHAPTER 43

Captain Underwood had very unsettling news for me early this morning. Breanne Jackson was dead. Marx was going to survive but would take several weeks to fully heal. James was under arrest but did post bail. No surprise because Monica had called to make the arrangements the day before. Underwood was going to allow James to see me but only under his supervision. He would be in sometime within the next hour. James' attorney would also be present.

After the briefing by Underwood, I asked about Branch. "Captain, did Branch make it?" I asked almost not wanting the answer.

"Her situation is still critical. All we know is that she is still alive," Underwood said quickly. "That's all I can really say."

"Well, let me know if something changes. You know the story and even though I know she is crazy, I still wouldn't wish death on anyone. It's hard to put some of this away right now."

"I understand," he said as he walked out of the room.

What I felt was real. What I went through was real. I thought of her steel blue eyes, her walk, and her calm confidence. I thought of how I just knew this would be different and that maybe someone really cared for me. I was fooled, and I thought what possibly could have made this woman come unhinged? Why am I so gullible to think someone will ever care for me? I think it's time to give up on that. I don't choose well.

About a half hour later, James, Captain Underwood and James' attorney came to my room. I was so glad to see James and that he was out. He was going to be under supervision and protection, but at least he wasn't behind bars. We weren't able to talk about the case and what had happened. We just could only have small talk. At least I could see him and that he was okay. He was my brother and we were always close. He had saved my life and I had always seen a heroic person in him. We chatted for about fifteen minutes and then he had to go. It was good to have him here, but I knew he needed to be with Monica and the kids. We said our goodbyes and I knew we were in for a long year. This process would wear us all down. I was hoping for a quick end to this nightmare. I was fooled, tricked, kidnapped and beaten. I have issues, bad ones. This can only be the start of the repair of a life that was always in need of repair. On the balance scale, I could never seem to find the middle that was the true sign of contentment.

Right at this moment, I could only think of those who I put in this awful situation. I held out hope for Katy and her return to her life. The scars would remain, but what about the feelings she has for me?

Somehow it is hard to return those feelings. It's just not the way I feel about her. I don't want to hurt her or let her down, but I also can't solve my own problems rescuing someone else. I hoped that James would not be charged and he could resume his life with his family.

In my mind I also prayed for Margaret, who had lost the only important people in her life. She had come to the hospital to see me. I could tell she wasn't doing well. She had received all of Sheila's things from her apartment and had tried to go through them, piece by piece. With every box she opened, she was hoping to find some reason for Sheila's death. She knew in her heart that Sheila would not kill herself.

▲

I had it bad for Branch. I couldn't help but wonder all the things she had experienced in life that had made her into the person she was. It was the grace with which she walked and the eyes that held me that kept telling me this couldn't have possibly happened. But it did happen. I wanted her to live, but for what reason I didn't know. It didn't make sense. It seems like I just want an imaginary relationship. One I could change anytime I felt pressured by it. Leave it when I needed to get away, and then return when all was well. That's not what it would take for me to be a better person. I just had some things I needed to face. Here I was once again, back to the beginning. I see hurdles, lots of them...

▲

Underwood came back to my room and told me that Allison Branch was going to survive. I sighed just a bit and for some strange reason I was relieved. For many days and many nights, Allison Branch would be a part of my world to come. I really don't know what to think. This next year will be the hardest year of my life. I have no idea what is going to happen, but every one of my senses said it was all going to be difficult. One door closes and another opens. You never know exactly what it is that you are going to find beyond the next open door. Sometimes you can only put one foot ahead of the other and take the next step. Where it is going to lead...I really don't know. I needed something. Something to lead me.

CHAPTER 44

*"The world is mine it can be yours my friend, so why
don't you pretend?"*
Nat King Cole, "Pretend"

Six months later...

The depositions were taken, the attorneys are seated and the trial is about to begin. The healing process for all the wounded like Marx, Katy, James and me had happened to the point where we all felt we could go on and begin the trial. It would last for the next three months.

The healing process for Branch was a different story. She was brought to the courtroom handcuffed and shackled, just as she had been emotionally all her life. It was hard to imagine the true complexities of the human mind when it is being led down a road of one bizarre moment after another. Branch had been motivated highly to be successful. So much so, she had a warped sense of how you get to that pinnacle. For some people in this world, a few lives affected here and there have no meaning or create no conscience. It's like living on Greed Street, driving on Narcissistic Road and ending up at Selfish Place, roads she had been driven all her life, roads that she was familiar with. She never had any regret or responsibility. She also lived in several dark areas in her mind. There were areas that many people dare not reside. Rejection and failure are not always handled easily by most people in general. But for Allison Branch, failure and rejection were like demons that jumped out at her from the darkness. Those demons told her what to do when she failed or when someone would not choose her. The eyes that used to feel like they had captured all of me were now fiercely dark and evil. I just had to look away.

The trial lasted for the next three months. The result was the sentencing of Allison Branch to 30 years in prison and no parole. It was exhausting and the relief when it ended was somewhat overshadowed by the funny way I felt sorry for her. When they led her out of the courtroom, I felt bad for her, but yet knew just how evil she was. The defense had tried to plead insanity, but the jury did not buy it. Her expert witnesses were debunked by the prosecutors and although she has a lot of problems, insanity wasn't proven. Just as quickly as she had strolled into my life, she was gone. She would be incarcerated at the Federal Corrections Institution at Oxford, Wisconsin.

▲

After the trial I stopped by to see Katy at her place. She had been going to a psychologist for three months now. She had improved significantly and we felt we were ready to have the conversations that we had needed to have long ago. As I walked into her living room, we both sat in chairs facing each other. Her face was showing a look of peacefulness that I hadn't seen in her for some time.

"It's good to see you again," I began nervously. Saying the right things would be crucial so I was being careful. "I know you have been through a lot and my timing may be off here, but let's think through this situation that we have been through."

Katy's face was somewhat quizzical as I sat more forward in my chair. "You have to know that you have been one of my best friends for the past five years. I can't think of anyone, outside of James, that I have shared more of my personal life with," I continued. "I know what you have said, and you have told me what you feel. I understand and respect that. But as hard as this is to say, I have to say it. I think the world of you. You're smart, pretty and we went through a rough experience where you helped pull us through. Not wanting to hurt you, I do need to say that my feelings for you are deep, but they are not the same for you and me."

Crystal tears began to fall from her eyes. *Damn, I knew this was going to be hard.* "I know, Mike. I wanted it to be us. I tried so hard to get you to love me just the same way I loved you," she said as she rose from her chair to stand by me. She laid her hand on my shoulder and said, "I do understand, my heart doesn't want to accept it, but I have to and move on. You will always be that one man who could draw me to him like a magnet. I needed you, I still do. But I will try to let go of those thoughts and move on. But I think that will be hard to do."

I stood and took hold of both of her hands and faced her. With tears streaming down her face, her eyes were telling me it would be okay, I hugged her and held her close, wishing that I could love her like she wanted me to. "Katy, you will always be a special person to me. I will hold you in a special place in my heart for as long as I breathe." Her face was buried in my chest and I stroked her hair gently. I knew I had to go now, before anything else I said would be misinterpreted. "We will still be friends, right? I can still come to the bar and have our conversations?"

"Sure, Mike, sure," she said although I really don't know at this time if even that was a good idea.

"I love you and what we have been through together will always keep us friends for life," as I stood looking at her wanting to not feel so awkward. But, it is always what I feel. Awkward. I turned to leave and as I walked down the hallway with her, she led me to the front door and opened it. I started to walk out and she said, "You know, I will always love you..."

And with that, I was once again alone. Awkward and alone. Back to the place where I seem to always start. I think Katy would have preferred if I fell madly in love, head over heels, with her. The world was hers could be ours, if only I could pretend. I just couldn't.

CHAPTER 45

It's Saturday and today I will be making my first trip to the lake house since all the terrible things that had happened. I have been reluctant to be there and conjure up the nightmares. But, I wanted to try and face it. There was so much to reflect on, Allison Branch, James, Katy, Brenda, Margaret, Marx and, of course, my awkward self.

The drive was peaceful enough, and the summer breeze was going to be nice. I had gotten a new boat, a completely different boat and thought about taking a ride in it this afternoon. I would have a nice June day on the lake. I arrived at 10:00 am and walked up the steps, inserted the key, and walked inside. Not to my surprise, the place gave me the feeling that what I had feared, then and now, was going to be hard to overcome. I could feel the tension I had felt when Branch held Katy hostage. The room smelled of fear and anxiety. Okay, maybe this wasn't the time yet. But I had to do something, to put this away for now.

Maybe the boat ride? I finished unpacking and was glad to be going outside and taking in the fresh air. This will be hard to kick. I took the golf cart down to the dock and suddenly the air and the sun seemed to fix what was wrong with me temporarily. I am a water person, I love being on the lake. I got in the boat and started out from the dock and headed out of my cove to the open lake.

The wind, that blew in my face, was refreshing as it seemed to take the events of the past year with it. I felt clean again. My mind was open to re-thinking my own life and to finally becoming the kind of person I thought I could be.

I stopped the boat in my favorite cove and just drifted for a while. The cool June breezes were making the day seem satisfying, mentally and physically. It is the beginning of an adjustment and reconciliation of all that has happened to me. It would now be time to make decisions in a life tainted with bad ones.

Sometimes when things happen in lives that are unexpected, you have to learn to roll with it somehow. My need to make some things right doesn't allow me to change what has happened. The hard lessons in life are that indeed...hard. But even in the midst of what I called the black cloud or bad karma, I still needed to fight for the person that I have to be.

The boat rocked back and forth from the waves of a few other boaters on the lake. For the most part I am alone. For right now, that is what I need. I still need to do this alone and without help. My mind tells me this is so.

I look at my watch and it is 4:00 pm. Time to head back and fight the one last demon and that would be staying in that house and being able to sleep. I head back to the dock, raise the boat on my lift and make sure all the systems are turned off. The lake has been good for me today. I stand on the dock and look out at the safest place I know. It is the water. It always has been and always will be my sanctuary. To the east, I see the darkness begin to place the shadow on the beginning of night. To the west, I see the setting sun of another day gone by. I hate to walk away from one of the most beautiful times of the day, but I have to know if I can stay in this place. Going up the path to my house, I am remembering what Katy and I went through, trying to find James, and witnessing a horrid scene near my house and inside of it.

Of course, that thinking brought me back to Branch. I continued walking towards my house and to the back porch. I slowly shuffled to the steps and looked up. I couldn't lift my feet. I could see Branch and Breanne holding Katy and making me give up my gun. I saw in her there the same eyes that I saw in the courtroom, eyes of deceit, hate, and anger. Her face drawn and her mind determined to get her piece of destiny.

I turned to walk away, but I stopped and scolded myself. *Face it. Don't be a coward. It's the only way to take back your life is to fight. You can walk away or just get up the steps and get in there and take your house back, take your sanity back, and take the first step to redemption. You have to do this.* I turned back and climbed the steps to the back porch and let myself in and then did something I never did before out here at the lake house. I locked the door.

CHAPTER 46

*You can't understand the cloud that follows me
around, and I can't explain what I don't know myself.
But if you believe sorrow and pain can't coexist with
happiness, that I can't smile without true joy if I am
depressed, that the sun can't shine while it's pouring
rain, and there are no shades of grey...If you don't
believe the truth can be told from a liar's lips, then
you don't understand life, and I don't have time to
explain myself.*
-Alicia N. Green

I woke up Sunday with just a few hours of sleep. Maybe it will get better, but I did stay here and that was the first hurdle. I went to the kitchen and made a cup of coffee and went to the front porch. I sat in the Adirondack chair and set my coffee on the side table.

At this moment, I had no idea what was in store for me. Life moving forward will be challenging, but I think in many ways I am beginning to see a light at the end of the tunnel. I think of Katy often and how I left her house that day. I haven't been back to the bar since that day. I see James on various occasions.

Marx had called me a couple of times to see if I would be interested in working with the department in violent crime cases. I told him I was flattered, but, right now, I would just keep teaching at the college. It was the safe thing for me to do. I needed to get away from the violent crimes thing. Marx and I were becoming friends though and we talked often. As much as I hated the guy in the beginning, I realized just how smart of a cop he was. The conversations never went to Branch. I think we both stayed away from that one. I think we both were fooled, but, of course, me more than him. *Be careful who you trust...*

James and Monica were back to as normal a life as I knew those two strong people would accomplish. James is a rock to me, my best friend, and we will spend many more days fishing the waters of the lake and having a few beers in the evenings. If I know one thing for sure, when the going is rough, you can always count on family. If I stop and think really hard most days, I can always find one piece of my past with family that can make me smile and also find that I would really miss each one if they were gone. With James, that will always hold true.

It's funny how time can fly when you are thinking deeply. The minutes that go by seem like hours of dreams and imaginary conversations you have with the important people in your life. It is now 4:00 pm and I am packed and ready to go back to the city. Someday I will be here and find someone to share this place. Someday, redemption of my soul will come full circle and I will be as happy as I can be and be depressed no longer. No more bad karma, no more black clouds to interrupt my life. They will be reduced to just challenges and hurdles, but they will be things I can conquer.

Allison Branch was pacing in her room at the Medical Rehabilitation Prison. She hated Mike Parsons deeply, even more than she hated her partner, Andy Marx. Branch, the Voice, and Breanne had made the perfect plan. It was ruined by those jerks. Allison is caged. When she is caged, Allison is her most dangerous self. Rejected by Parsons and always one-upped by Marx, she also had endured the rejection by society as well and she was going to be treated like an animal. She could not have this. She sat on the end of her bed filled with rage. So much so, that tears of sheer anger dropped from her eyes to her hospital gown. She was going to get them all. She would need a plan.

_____▲_____

I arrived back at my condo around six that evening. Tomorrow is a work day and I had taken my normal routine back. After unpacking, I sat on the back deck with a scotch and water.

Redemption is many things and may take many forms. It can be clearing a debt, being saved from sin and error, or regaining the possession of something. But the terms of redemption may not be savory and the debt is sometimes what a person is unwilling to pay. My own redemption will take payment and atonement. But I think I am willing to pay the dues required.

To see into one's own soul is one thing. To see deeply into someone else's is entirely something else.

If anything, the search for my redemption has delivered me to, at the very least, a place where I can begin again. Fortunately, my mind says this is not the end and I have chosen for it to be the beginning. Freeing me from guilt and self-pity has been enlightening. My deliverance back to home plate with a new set of no balls and no strikes to start this at bat, has given my life some new meaning. I can't know if I will succeed or fail, but I am ready to fight. Life is worth fighting for and the demons that are there can be defeated, but you have to fight.

Made in the USA
Las Vegas, NV
15 February 2023

67559117R10105